A GROOM FOR GRETA

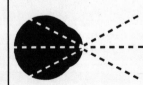

This Large Print Book carries the
Seal of Approval of N.A.V.H.

AMISH BRIDES OF CELERY FIELDS

A GROOM FOR GRETA

ANNA SCHMIDT

THORNDIKE PRESS
A part of Gale, Cengage Learning

 GALE
CENGAGE Learning·

Detroit • New York • San Francisco • New Haven, Conn • Waterville, Maine • London

GALE
CENGAGE Learning®

LIBRARY OF CONGRESS CATALOGING-IN-PUBLICATION DATA

Schmidt, Anna, 1943–
  A Groom For Greta / By Anna Schmidt. — Large Print edition.
    pages cm. — (Amish Brides of Celery Fields Series) (Thorndike Press Large Print Gentle Romance)
  ISBN 978-1-4104-6412-5 (hardcover) — ISBN 1-4104-6412-1 (hardcover)
  1. Amish—Fiction. 2. Courtship—Fiction. 3. Large type books. I. Title.
PS3569.C51527G76 2013
813'.54—dc23   2013030310

Published in 2013 by arrangement with Harlequin Books S.A.

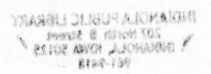
Printed in the United States of America
1 2 3 4 5 6 7 17 16 15 14 13

But you delight in sincerity of heart and in secret you teach me wisdom

For Larry

CHAPTER ONE

Celery Fields, Florida
Summer 1934

Luke Starns hammered the molten iron into shape, the sound of metal on metal ringing in his ears as the hammer struck the rod. He set the half-completed horseshoe on the white-hot fire and wiped his brow with the back of his bare forearm. Then he stretched as he pushed open the single window that offered relief from the shadowy darkness of his blacksmith shop and livery stable. He was hoping for a breeze, but this was Florida, not Ontario. And it was August, steamy and humid, and at four in the afternoon there was no sign of relief from the oppressive heat. He fanned himself with the wide-brimmed straw hat that was one of the unmistakable signs of his Amish heritage.

Business was slow but not nearly as slow as it was in the outside world — the rest of

Florida. The economic depression that had gripped the entire United States had taken a huge toll on businesses and lives all across the state. Luke counted himself fortunate that he had skills that were still in demand — although with the growing number of cars and trucks crowding the roads, he wasn't sure how long there would be enough customers to sustain his business.

He thought about taking a break, perhaps getting a dish of ice cream at the parlor next to the bakery. He wasn't exactly dressed for shopping but it was late on a Saturday. Most everyone living in and around the Amish settlement of Celery Fields would have already headed home. As he rolled down the sleeves to his collarless shirt, he heard voices just outside the small window — a man and a woman — the man's voice was stern and serious, the woman's laughter was high-pitched and nervous.

"I can't marry you, Greta Goodloe," the man announced. Luke sighed. Quarrels between Greta and her long-time beau, Josef Bontrager, were so common that most of the townspeople tended to ignore them completely. Luke was inclined to agree that this was probably the best plan. He finished rolling down his sleeves and glanced out the window when he heard the soft plod of horse hooves in the sandy street and saw Bontrager's dark buggy driving away. After that all was quiet.

Wiping his hands — black with the soot of his work — on a rag he kept hanging by the window, he removed his leather apron and checked the front of his homespun cotton shirt. Then he ran his fingers through his damp black hair and reached for his hat. A dish of Jeremiah Troyer's vanilla ice cream was sounding better and better, but he wanted to at least make the effort to look decent before venturing out. His concern was not for himself, but he felt it was just good manners to make the effort for others. He was headed for the door of his shop when he heard a sound.

The two double doors to his blacksmith shop and livery stood fully ajar but there was no one there. At least that he could see. Then he heard the sound again. A soft keening like someone in pain. He moved closer to the door's opening and there framed in the doorway, cast in silhouette by the late afternoon sun at her back, stood a woman — an unwed Amish woman, given the black ties of her prayer *kapp* that peeked out from beneath her bonnet. She was grasping the frame of the doorway.

Fearing that she had been struck ill or

perhaps overcome by the heat, Luke rushed forward. On his way he grabbed the shop's one battered chair. "Hold on," he ordered, but before he could reach her, she took two steps forward and then started to crumple to the floor. Luke dropped the chair and caught the woman.

"What's to become of me?" she whispered as she looked up at him from beneath the brim of her bonnet with fathomless sea blue eyes that belonged to only one female in Celery Fields.

Greta Goodloe.

"Are you ill, Greta Goodloe?" he asked, raising his voice in case she might be on the verge of passing out. "Wounded? Have you been in an accident?"

"Oh, he's broken it," she moaned miserably, her voice choking on her sobs.

"Who? What is broken?"

She looked up at him, her eyes widening in what he could only describe as horror. With surprising strength for one so petite, she pushed him away and stood without support for the first time since entering his shop. She glanced around and seemed stunned to find herself there, but she no longer appeared to be in danger of passing out.

"Sit down," Luke ordered, sliding the

chair behind her. "Let me have a look. Is it your . . ." He ran through the possibilities. She was standing without apparent pain on both legs. Her arms were flailing about like windmills as she apparently tried to regain control of her emotions. "Where is the pain, Greta Goodloe?" he shouted, hoping to break through what was clearly a case of hysteria.

"Right here," she announced, clutching at her chest. "And please stop shouting. Do you want the whole town to witness my . . ." Fresh tears leaked down her cheeks and she sat down hard in the chair and buried her face in her hands as her entire body shuddered with the force of her crying.

She was awfully young for a heart attack but he seemed to recall that her father had died of one a year or so earlier and her mother had succumbed to heart failure when Greta was but a toddler. If it ran in the family . . .

"Stay there. I'll go for the doctor."

She was on her feet in an instant and looking mighty healthy for a woman having palpitations. "You will do no such thing," she growled. "You will have the decency to forget that I ever came in here today, that you ever witnessed . . ." Once again her eyes filled with fresh tears. "My shame," she whispered and sat down on the chair.

Only this time she did not fall to pieces as Luke might have expected. Instead she looked all around the shop, finally settling her gaze on him. Then she drew in a heavy sigh and fixed him with a look that seemed rather harsh, considering he had done nothing more than show her kindness and concern.

"So, Luke Starns, we have a problem. That is, I have a problem — several of them at the moment. But let's begin with addressing the problem before you and me."

"I'm listening," he replied. "I'll help if I can but I'm not sure what . . ."

"Oh, please do not pretend that you weren't eavesdropping just now," she snapped. "I saw you standing by that window there. You had to have heard and seen every horrible bit of it."

Luke frowned. "And I am telling you that whatever might have taken place between you and Josef Bontrager . . ."

"There," she interrupted pointing her finger at him, "you admit it. You were watching us. I have not so much as mentioned Josef's name and still you . . ."

Luke had no time and little patience for her tantrum. "You are speaking in riddles, Greta Goodloe. This is my establishment

14

and if I take a moment from my work to stand at my window that is my right."

"Your window is open as are your doors. Do you honestly expect me to believe that you did not hear my conversation with Josef?"

"I cannot say what you will believe or not. I am telling you that whatever business you had just now with Josef is of no interest to me. And now if you are feeling better I have work to do." He abandoned the idea of ice cream and headed back toward the fire. But given that Greta Goodloe was right there next to him when he turned to pick up his apron, it was evident that this was not yet over.

He was dismissing her. Greta was certain that the blacksmith had heard and seen everything. When Josef had driven away, she'd seen Luke Starns watching from his window — the window that overlooked the town's main and only street. Her intent in entering the shadowy recesses of his shop had been to confront him and make sure that he did not speak of what he had seen to anyone else. For surely Josef's announcement was some nightmare from which she would awaken any moment.

One minute she and Josef Bontrager —

the man she would finally marry after five long years of courtship — were looking at a china teapot in Yoder's Dry Goods. The next they were crossing the street on their way to the lane that led past the blacksmith and livery stables and on to the small house that Greta shared with her older sister, Lydia.

Suddenly Josef had stopped walking and when she had turned back to him, her chatter about plans for their wedding momentarily silenced, Josef had looked down at his dusty boots and said the very last thing she could ever have imagined coming from his mouth.

"I cannot marry you, Greta Goodloe."

At first Greta's mind had raced with any possible cause for Josef's unbelievable declaration. "You mean this autumn?"

Tradition had it that marriages took place in late autumn after the fall harvest. At least that had been the way of things up north where most of the Florida Amish had lived before migrating to Celery Fields. Of course, in Florida late autumn was just when the planting started. The following day at services, Bishop Troyer would announce all the weddings that would take place that fall.

So Greta and Josef had planned their wedding for September to give themselves plenty of time to travel north for the traditional round of visits with family and friends. They'd be back in time to plant the fields of celery, the cash crop on the large farm that Josef had taken over when his father and brothers decided to move back north.

"I mean I know times have been hard," she had rushed to add, wanting to assure Josef that in spite of his constant worries over financial matters, they would be fine. He was always talking about the depression and how even though business in Celery Fields had not been affected, there could come a time when the community would feel the ravages of the financial disaster sweeping the rest of the country.

"I suppose that we could wait one more year," she added, hoping to find some way to quell his worries. She would be twenty-three by then, almost as old as Lydia was now. But still if Josef thought it best to wait . . .

Josef's features had been shadowed by the brim of his hat. "This isn't about hard times, Greta." He sucked in air as if he'd been underwater for far too long. "Well, there's that, of course, but what I mean to say, Greta, is that I can't marry you — ever."

"Oh, Josef, is this because you saw me

talking to the Hadwells' cousin last week?"

Josef snorted and transferred his gaze from the ground to the sky, still refusing to look directly at her. "You certainly seemed to be enjoying your time with him."

"So, you're jealous." Relief mixed with irritation flooded her veins. This was not the first time that Josef had been upset with her for what he saw as flirting and she saw as simply being herself. "The Hadwells' cousin has gone back home to Indiana," she pointed out.

"There will be others," Josef muttered.

Greta counted to ten. How many times had she reassured this man over the course of their lives together? How many more times would she have to apologize for being herself? She closed her eyes and prayed for guidance — and patience.

"Well," she replied with a smile that felt as if it might actually make her face crack, "if that is your decision . . ." And with a toss of her head she had continued on across the street. She'd been so certain that Josef would come after her. He always did. He would apologize. She would accept his apology and reassure him that he was the one for her and that would be that.

She had almost reached the blacksmith shop before she realized that Josef was not coming after her. Indeed after a moment she heard the jingle of harness and the creak of buggy wheels headed out of town. He had left her. Her step faltered. Her mind had reeled with the possible options of where she might go. She could have gone to the school where Lydia would be preparing lessons for her students for the coming week. She could have gone to the bakery where her half sister, Pleasant, would also be preparing to close up shop for the day, or to Bishop Troyer's house where his wife, Mildred, would undoubtedly offer her a sympathetic ear and a nice cold glass of lemonade.

That's when she looked up and saw Luke Starns, the dark mysterious man who had shown up in Celery Fields just a few months earlier, standing at his window. He must have seen and heard everything. In an instant she had retraced her steps, determined to set Luke Starns straight about minding his own business.

But when she had reached the open doorway of Luke's business, she had caught a glimpse of Josef's buggy disappearing in a cloud of dust and the full force of what had just happened had hit her like a blow to her stomach. For one horrible instant she could not seem to breathe and her knees had turned to jam. She had grasped the rough door frame for support and barely noticed as a splinter pierced her thumb.

Now as the blacksmith loomed over her — all six feet and more of him — she sucked at her injured thumb and considered her options.

"Do you have a cut?" Luke asked, nodding toward her hand.

Greta instantly ripped her thumb from her mouth and curled her other fingers around it. "No. It's a splinter — from your doorway," she added as if he had purposefully left the offending object there to wound her.

"Let me look at it," he said as he gently took hold of her hand and coaxed her fingers open. Then he held her hand closer to the light of the fire, examined the wound and frowned.

For her part Greta was taken aback at the contrast of her hand — small and very white — resting on his rougher, larger, burnished palm. He reached for a pail of clear water with a tin dipper resting in it and trickled a little of the cooling water over her thumb. Fascinated in spite of her determination to maintain her focus on the larger problems at hand, Greta watched as with surprising dexterity for one with such thick fingers he worked free the splinter.

"There," he said, and the word came out as if he'd been holding his breath until the deed was done. He released her hand. Filling the dipper with fresh water, he offered it to her. "Drink this."

She did as he asked, more to buy time than because she was thirsty. She found that the absence of his hand holding hers was troubling — as if she had been deprived of something precious. It was a ridiculous idea of course. She was simply missing the absence of Josef's touch. This had nothing to do with Luke Starns, nothing at all.

"Denki," she said, thanking him as she drank the water then handed back the dipper. She waited until he had turned to set the bucket back in its place before adding, "I want to set your mind at ease but first I must know how much you overheard?"

"Bitte?"

"Of the disagreement between Josef and me," she reminded him. When he said nothing, she added, "We seem to have a lot of those these days."

Luke remained silent.

"Nerves, I expect — for both of us," Greta explained, warming to her tale. This earned her a flicker of curiosity from the blacksmith's deep-set eyes.

"The wedding?" she reminded him. *Men.*

How could they be so incredibly thickheaded about the important events of life?

She glanced toward the street and across the way she saw her half sister, Pleasant, locking up the bakery for the night. Her conversation with Josef had taken place right out in the open where anyone might have seen or heard — not just Luke Starns. Panicked anew at the thought of others witnessing the scene, Greta made a quick inventory of the businesses along the street. Yoder's Dry Goods where Hilda Yoder was known to keep an eye on everything that might happen in town. But three local women had passed by Josef and Greta as they left the shop. So Hilda would have been busy serving her customers when Josef made his astounding announcement.

The hardware store next door to the blacksmith's? Roger Hadwell and his wife, Gertrude, were known gossips but neither of them had been in evidence when Josef made his stunning pronouncement. Greta breathed a little easier and decided that she only had to worry about the blacksmith. She studied him for a long moment, trying to decide on her best strategy. Charm had always been her most potent weapon for getting herself out of any tight spot. But would charm work on this man?

Luke Starns was not someone she had had the opportunity to get to know. The truth was that she had kept her distance from him. There was something about him that stirred a shyness in her that simply was not there with anyone else. Perhaps it was his looks. Where most of the men in Celery Fields — as well as the women — were fair with white-blond hair and skin that freckled easily, Luke Starns was dark — his hair was as black as the leather apron he wore to do his work. His skin was deeply tanned as if he spent his days outdoors instead of hunched over a roaring fire hammering bridle bits and horseshoes into shape. And his eyes were set deep under a brow of thick black eyebrows and were the most unexpected shade of blue — like cornflowers, Greta had thought the first time she'd seen him at services.

Of course, from the minute he'd arrived in Celery Fields, every woman in town had begun planning a match for him. Theirs was a small community and that meant that the available number of eligible men for every single female in the town was limited. The preferred candidate for Luke Starns was Greta's sister, Lydia. But Lydia had dismissed such idle speculation as she had all hints that this man or that might make a good match for her.

"Don't you want to marry?" Greta had asked.

"Yes, that would be nice. But I will not settle, sister. I'd rather spend my days alone."

Now Greta shuddered in spite of the oppressive heat of the August day. The very idea that in the face of Josef's abandonment she might now spend *her* days alone was beyond her ability to comprehend. How would she survive? What would she do? Lydia had her students who adored her, but Greta — what did she have? Practically her entire life, everyone had simply assumed that one day she would marry Josef, keep house for him in the impressive farmhouse that set on the edge of town, and fill that house with babies.

That had been the plan — until twenty minutes ago.

She felt Luke watching her now. There was not a single reason to think he had any interest in what had happened between Josef and her. *Oh, the sin of conceit,* she thought as she stood up and pressed her hands over her green cotton skirt — the one that Josef had always liked.

"The wedding?" Luke prompted her now.

Greta pasted on a smile that came as

naturally to her as breathing. "I am quite aware that you may believe that what you witnessed between Josef and me earlier was unusual. I assure you that it was not. Josef is having an attack of nerves, nothing more."

He frowned. "*Yah,* you are probably right."

"I am right," she assured him and almost believed it herself. "So there is no need for you to concern yourself with my . . ."

"Might this mean that Josef Bontrager will not be available to drive you and your sister to services tomorrow then?" he asked.

The idea had not yet occurred to Greta. Oh, the ripples this thing was going to have if Josef didn't come to his senses before morning. She was barely aware that Luke had continued speaking, so caught up was she in the ramifications Josef's fit of pique might have.

"Because if that is the case then I would be pleased to drive you — and Lydia Good-loe. It is on my way."

As she forced her attention back to the blacksmith, Greta bristled. The man had some nerve. "Luke Starns, it has not been yet half an hour since the man I thought for years I would wed has broken with me. And you want me to set all that aside so you can court me in his stead?"

25

She saw him stiffen with wounded pride. It was a male trait that she was well familiar with. After all, she'd observed it numerous times in Josef.

"*Neh,* Greta Goodloe." He held up both hands as if to ward off such an unpleasant thought.

He didn't have to look quite so repulsed, Greta thought. "Forgive me," she said. "I misunderstood. It has been . . ."

But Luke did not allow her to finish her apology before blurting out, "It is not you but your sister that I wish to call upon."

And suddenly the events of the day seemed far too ridiculous to be real. Were the tables to be turned so that Lydia was the one to be courted and wed while Greta spent her days alone? She couldn't help herself. She started to laugh and could not seem to stop.

"Lydia?" Greta finally managed to form the word. "You have finally found your nerve and set your sights on Lydia?"

"I have." Everything about his posture challenged her to dispute his decision.

"My sister is not seeking a match," Greta warned. But the more Greta thought about it, the better the idea seemed to her. Why shouldn't Lydia find happiness even if Greta herself seemed doomed to eternal spinsterhood? After all, everyone in town had speculated that the best possible match for the blacksmith would be Lydia. For months now the local gossips had been waiting for Luke to make his move. Apparently he had finally decided to do so. "On the other hand, perhaps she has not considered every available candidate." She walked around him, studying him carefully. "Would you consider a bargain?"

"A bargain?"

"Yes. I will do what I can to help in your campaign to win my sister's affection. And in return, you will say nothing to anyone about what you observed earlier between Josef and me."

He sighed wearily. "How many times must I say this? I heard nothing. I did see you with Josef outside my window as I have seen the two of you and many other people in town numerous times before. I cannot be responsible for what takes place on the other side of the glass, Greta."

"Yes or no," she challenged. "I can be more influential than you may suspect in whether or not Lydia takes your attentions seriously."

Luke chuckled. "Why, Greta Goodloe, are you threatening me?"

"Not at all. After all, I have no control

over what you may do with whatever information you gathered while observing Josef and me earlier." She fought to keep her voice steady. It was very important to her that the whole town should not know the embarrassing circumstances of Josef's sudden decision to call off their engagement. She looked up at Luke, wondering if she could trust this relative stranger to hold his tongue when the gossip began — as it surely would. "Please," she whispered.

"Very well. We have a bargain, Greta. One I fully intend to see that you keep. I will call for you and your sister tomorrow morning and . . ."

But Greta had lost interest in the conversation as she once again faced the fact that after five years of courtship — on the eve of the announcement of their plans to wed — Josef Bontrager had quit her. She sank down onto the chair and buried her face in her hands as the tears flowed anew with no sign of stopping.

CHAPTER TWO

Luke was willing to admit that his offer to drive the Goodloe sisters to services had been a spur-of-the-moment idea. For a good part of the day, he'd been trying to think of some way that he might approach Lydia Goodloe. He wanted to ask her if he could see her home from the Sunday evening singing that served as an opportunity for the single population of Celery Fields to socialize and court.

Circumstances in his past had forced Luke to make some major changes in his life. The first had been to leave Ontario and move here to Celery Fields where he knew no one — and more to the point, no one knew him. The second was to settle here permanently and that meant taking a wife. Now that his business was established, if not exactly flourishing, and he seemed to have been accepted by others in the community, it was time to marry and start his family. He was twenty-seven years old. By his age his parents had already had him plus three brothers.

Then just as he was planning his strategy for how best to approach Lydia, Greta Goodloe had suddenly appeared in his doorway and the way had seemed clear to him. If he could enlist her aid in courting her sister . . .

But after interacting with Greta over these last several moments, he was having second thoughts about involving her in his quest. At first the woman had been nearly hysterical. Then she had accused him of eavesdropping — no, spying — on her private conversation with Josef and when he had told her of his intent to court her sister, her mood had once again shifted. She had actually burst out laughing. He certainly saw no cause for such merriment — at his expense.

Now she was back to crying again — crying so hard that she had begun to hiccup. For the life of him Luke would never understand women. Not that he was all that used to being around women in the first place. His mother had died when he was just six and his younger brothers and father had been his world until he'd left the family home in Ontario this last spring. Blacksmithing was his trade, which did not bring him into much contact with the female of the species. That had worked out fine for him so far.

It occurred to him that a woman like Greta — a woman well known for her charm and beauty throughout the community — might logically assume that any man would be attracted to her. That explained her reaction when he'd offered the ride to Sunday services. And Luke had to admit that when he'd first begun to consider the single women of Celery Fields, he had — as any man would — taken notice of Greta Goodloe.

She had a smile that was as filled with sunshine as her golden hair — at least what he could see of her hair bound tightly beneath the covering of her black bonnet. And she was not the least bit shy about spreading the sunshine of that smile around. More than once he'd been working and had heard her musical laughter as she passed by his shop on her way home or to do some shopping at Yoder's.

But he'd quickly learned that she and Josef Bontrager were together. In fact it was the idea that Greta would soon wed, leaving Lydia in her late parents' house alone with no further responsibilities for her sister that had made him take closer notice of the teacher.

From what Luke had observed, Lydia was her younger sister's opposite in just about every way. Greta was petite with a natural beauty. Her sister was attractive but her height and angular features gave her an aura of authority and more than a little intimidation. Luke supposed that suited a schoolteacher who needed to maintain order and control over children of a variety of ages. But away from school she was still wary and withdrawn when it came to socializing with others — especially those she did not know. Greta, on the other hand, was outgoing to the point of being a bit adventurous. Her ready smile and lively eyes reflected an innate curiosity about people. One more reason, Luke had decided, that he should set his sights on the quieter, more steadfast Lydia.

Determined to get on with the matter of pursuing his courtship of Lydia, Luke was beginning to lose patience with the way Greta's mood could change from tears to laughter and back to tears with stunning quickness. But then she buried her face in her hands and her slim shoulders shuddered violently. "How is this possible?" she managed between hiccups.

"I believe that your sister and I would make . . ."

"Not that," she snapped, the hiccups apparently cured by her sudden fit of temper. She looked off toward the direction that Josef Bontrager had gone as silent tears flowed freely down her cheeks. "Oh, what's to become of me?" she moaned, wrapping her arms around herself.

"I expect you'll do fine," Luke said as he refilled the dipper and handed it to her. "You're young and from what I've observed there isn't an eligible man in town who . . ."

She looked up at him, her blue eyes wide with horror, her mouth working as if she wanted to say something but could not make her voice work. "You men think that it's . . . How dare you for one minute . . ." she stuttered and shoved the dipper into his hand. "Do not plan to call for us tomorrow for services, Luke Starns," she ordered, then turned and stalked off down the lane that led to the house she shared with her sister.

How dare I what? Try to console you? Treat your injured finger? Fetch you water?

"Women," Luke muttered as he strode back inside his shop, hooked the halter of the heavy leather apron over his head and started pounding out the iron that he'd left on the fire.

Through the next half hour as Luke continued his work, Greta's accusations stayed with him as did her tears. Clearly she remained convinced that he had passed judgment over whatever had passed between her and her beau. Still, thinking back on it, he realized that he'd been more aware of the disagreement than he'd fully understood. And the more he thought about the conversation he'd only partially paid attention to while he stood at the window, the harder he struck the iron on the anvil with extra force.

Josef Bontrager was a man given to the kind of bombastic announcements that carried above the normal sounds of a town going about its business. Though his announcement to Greta had come at the time of day when most folks had already gone home, his voice insured that anyone who happened to be nearby would hear what he had to say.

"I can't marry you, Greta."

No wonder the young woman had been so upset. This was no surely ordinary quarrel. The couple's plan to wed within a month was to be announced the following morning at services. If Bontrager meant what he'd said . . .

"*Guten tag,* Luke." Roger Hadwell stood

at the door of the shop, watching Luke pound the iron into shape. "You're working later than usual," he observed.

"*Yah.* Just finishing up here. Have some water." He nodded toward the bucket.

Roger helped himself while Luke made the last two strikes on the molten metal then shoved it into another bucket of water at his feet. Hot iron striking cold water produced the familiar sizzle of steam rising that Luke found somehow calming. "Come sit awhile," he invited. He followed Roger outside to the warped bench he kept ready for just such visits.

Roger owned the hardware business next door and frequently stopped by to exchange bits of news with Luke during the work-week. He was uncustomarily quiet as he sipped water from the dipper. "Did something happen to Greta Goodloe?" he asked finally.

Luke stalled for time. "Why do you ask?"

Roger shrugged. "Me and the wife couldn't help noticing that she stopped by your shop here after Josef drove off — and stayed a good little bit. My wife seemed to think that Greta was upset about something. She and Josef have another spat?"

Luke sent up a silent prayer for forgiveness for the lie he was about to tell. "It's the dust." He nodded toward the street where a hot westerly wind created little flurries of dirt and sand on the street. "Got something in her eye."

"That was it then," Roger said and Luke understood that this was a question.

"That and she'd gotten a splinter. I picked out the splinter and gave her some water. She took a few minutes to catch her breath and went on her way."

They sat watching Jeremiah and Pleasant Troyer pass, their buggy loaded with kids and the week's shopping. Pleasant nodded in greeting as Jeremiah turned the buggy toward home. The town would be pretty much deserted until everyone gathered at the Troyers' place the next day for services and the start of a new week.

"When I saw Greta and Josef earlier," Roger continued, "it looked like they were having words."

I can't marry you, Greta.

What kind of man just blurts out something like that in the middle of town where anybody might see or hear? What kind of man walks away without so much as an explanation for the woman he's professed to love for most of his life?

Luke couldn't imagine treating a woman — or any human being — with such callousness. He didn't know Greta Goodloe very well — really not at all other than seeing her in town or at services — but she seemed a kindhearted person and surely did not deserve such treatment from a man who had professed to love her. He thought about her smile and the way it could bring a special radiance to her features. But she had not been smiling much during the time she had spent in his shop.

He realized now that he'd gotten lost in thought while Roger had continued to speculate on what might have gone on between Greta and Josef. ". . . wouldn't be human if they didn't have words now and again. Whole town knows that this is hardly the first time. I mean you take a fiery little thing like Greta and put her with a man as fence-straddling as Josef and there are bound to be some times when they don't see eye to eye." He chuckled and stood up. "Wait 'til those two are married and spending all day and night together. Oh, there are gonna be some fireworks then, I'll guarantee it."

Roger was still chuckling to himself after he'd tipped his hat and sauntered back to the hardware store — no doubt to report to his wife that Luke had not had any further information to offer. Luke started inside his shop, but a flash of color caught his eye and he paused to look down the lane toward the house where the Goodloe sisters lived.

In the gathering dusk, Greta was taking down laundry from the clothesline that ran from the house to a palm tree and back again. She yanked free the clothespins and dropped them into a basket at her feet, then snapped the sheet, towel or clothing item hard against the hot westerly breeze and folded it into a precise rectangle before adding it to the pile already in another larger basket.

Luke told himself that he remained where he was watching her until the line was empty because he wanted to be sure that she had recovered from her earlier distress. But the truth was that he could not seem to stop watching her. It was as if Josef's harsh words had pried open a door. Suddenly the beautiful Greta Goodloe might be free to consider other suitors. And there had been a time when a much younger and more foolish Luke would have taken a good deal of pleasure in that news. But he had been different then.

"This is not the sister for you," he told himself sternly as he forced his gaze away from her and headed inside.

■ ■ ■ ■

Greta saw Luke Starns watching her. She'd also seen Roger Hadwell make his way over to the blacksmith's, observed the two men talking and wondered if Luke had decided that since she had already broken their bargain by refusing his offer of a ride to services, he was free to tell Roger everything. In that case she had made a complete fool of herself confiding in the blacksmith and, no doubt by morning, everyone in town was going to know about it. She would be the subject of whispers and conversations that stopped the moment she entered the room when she and Lydia arrived at services.

Oh, who do you think you're fooling? Sooner or later everyone has to know the whole story.

Well, let people talk. It certainly hadn't been her idea to end her relationship with Josef. And the way he had done it — in the middle of town, with no explanation at all? Of course, she really hadn't waited for him to explain. On the other hand, he could have followed her. But, oh no, he was too . . .

What?

Shy?

Proud?

39

Cowardly. Yes, that explained it. For as long as she'd known him, Josef had allowed her to have her way and deep down she had known that even the hint that she might be attracted to some other boy could have Josef falling all over himself to win favor with her. On the other hand, he had made it clear on more than one occasion that once they married, he would determine where she went and who she saw and when. Greta had accepted that, once she married, the man was in charge. But she had always assumed that after marriage she would be able to find her way around Josef's jealousies and strict ways the same way she had during their courtship.

She paused for a moment — a clothespin clinched between her lips — as she looked at Luke Starns. As usual she had acted in haste — confiding in him without thinking through the possible consequences. She barely knew the man beyond seeing him at services and the occasional nod when she passed his shop.

Honest. Trustworthy. These were words she'd heard applied to the blacksmith. But could she trust him? It had been evident that he failed to understand the seriousness of what had transpired between Josef and her — of just how precarious things were.

And yet he had listened and shown concern.

She had to trust someone. Perhaps he and Roger Hadwell had been discussing business or just passing the time of day. She would know tomorrow as soon as she and Lydia arrived at services. If Luke drove Lydia and her to services, as soon as they pulled into the yard of Pleasant's house, there would be one of two reactions. Either the women would be whispering about her and giving her those pitying looks that she could not abide. Or they would be talking about the surprise of seeing Lydia and Luke arrive together, delighted that at long last the romance they had all anticipated had taken its first baby step.

An idea began to take shape in her mind and she smiled softly to herself. She placed the last folded pillowcase on the pile of laundry. Arriving with Luke was definitely the way to go. If he had gossiped, she would know it at once and would then inform him that he was not worthy of Lydia and could certainly not depend on Greta to help him court her. If, on the other hand, he had held his tongue under the pressure of Roger's probing, then she could turn the attention of others to the prospect of a romance between Lydia and the blacksmith and all speculation about what had happened to her would be short-lived.

She hoisted the heavy basket onto one hip and headed back to the house. Somehow she had to get Lydia to agree to let Luke Starns drive them to services and see her home after the singing. While it would be nigh on to scandalous for Luke and Lydia to arrive for services without Greta's company, Sunday evening singings were occasions where single people in the community could openly socialize, even flirt a bit. Of course, in most Amish communities such gatherings were intended as events for young people in the sixteen to twenty age group. And in most Amish communities they attracted additional young people from surrounding Amish towns.

But Celery Fields was the sole Amish community for miles around in Florida and so these social evenings included anyone who was single — regardless of their age. Greta had never seen Luke at a singing in all the time he'd been in Celery Fields but clearly his intention was to be there the following evening. Now if indeed she found that she could trust Luke then all Greta had to do was make sure that he and Lydia were seated across from each other at the long table set up in the barn with the males on one side and the females on the other. And then she could make some excuse as to why she could not ride back to town with them.

Early on Sunday morning Greta heard Lydia stirring. Usually her sister would already have seen to the horse and cow they kept, gathered the eggs, prepared their breakfast and dressed in the lavender dress she reserved for their biweekly services, all before Greta was even out of bed. But not today.

Still smarting from the events of the day before, Greta had not slept well at all and she felt restless and out of sorts as she dressed. Using the blackened pins lined up on her bureau, she anchored her skirt into place. Then she twisted up her hair into a bun and pulled hairpins from between her lips to stab it into submission. Finally she lifted the prayer *kapp* from its resting place on her bedside table and prepared to set it atop the tight bun.

Unfortunately Lydia's answer to Greta's distress the evening before had been to counsel prayer, Scripture and early to bed. There had been no opportunity at all to bring up the subject of Luke Starns. Furthermore, in the middle of the night Greta had realized that because she had rejected Luke's offer to drive them after all, she needed to reverse that decision and hope that he would agree. Thus the urgency of her early morning errand — one that her sister must not observe.

Checking to be sure that Lydia was otherwise occupied, Greta picked up the note she'd prepared the night before and ran down the lane to the blacksmith shop. All was quiet through the little village and she thanked God for that. She crept up the staircase on the side of Luke's shop that led to his living quarters and slipped the envelope under the door. When she heard the distinctive sound of a man clearing his throat from somewhere beyond that door, she ran down the stairs and all the way back to her house.

Luke had found the small white envelope when he'd headed out to hitch up his wagon.

Luke Starns,
Your kind offer to drive my sister and me to services today is most appreciated. We will be ready at eight.
                            Greta Goodloe

Luke couldn't help but smile. So Greta Goodloe had decided to keep her end of their bargain after all. He wondered why. Greta did not strike him as a woman who did anything without a good reason — something that would be of benefit to her. Not that she wasn't devoted to her sister. Their closeness was well-known through Celery Fields and it was seldom that one was seen without the other — even when Josef Bontrager was around.

He reread the note. The implication was that Lydia had agreed to this idea — and that surprised Luke. More than surprised him, it made him suspicious. Had Greta actually gotten Lydia to agree to the plan? He doubted it. But now that he'd been given the opening he'd sought to call upon Lydia, he hardly cared what Greta's motives might be. Of far greater concern was that he return to his room above the shop and make sure that he had done everything he could to make the best possible impression on the schoolteacher.

He changed his shirt for one that he'd been saving for just such an occasion. He ran his thumbs down his suspenders making sure they were straight and without any twists. He brushed his navy wool pants to remove any possible traces of crumbs from his breakfast. Finally he picked up his wide-brimmed straw hat and set it precisely on his head, wishing for the first time in his life that he owned a mirror.

Pure vanity, he thought, chastising himself for such a lapse on the Sabbath of all days. He set his hat more firmly on his thick hair and headed downstairs to hitch up the wagon, thinking that it would be more proper if he had the courting buggy he'd been given when he had turned sixteen and left behind when he moved to Florida.

"Courting buggies are for kids," he muttered to the horses as he fixed them with their bits and harness. "Lydia Goodloe and I are no longer young. And she is a practical woman. She will not mind the wagon."

Outside he took special care hitching the team to the wagon and ran the flat of his hand over the seat to be sure there were no splinters that might catch on the sisters' skirts. He paused as he thought about the splinter he'd removed from Greta's thumb the day before. How vulnerable she had seemed standing there in the reflected light of the fire, licking at her wound like a kitten whose paw had been injured. How very smooth her skin had been especially in contrast to his rough and callused palms. For a moment he was carried back to Ontario — and another young woman whose hands had been as soft as that.

Luke shook off such thoughts. Those days were behind him. He lived here now. His life was here in Celery Fields and if God granted him his prayer, his future was with Lydia Goodloe — not her sister, no matter how pretty and lively she was.

Greta closed the door to her bedroom and sat on her bed, trying to catch her breath before going to share breakfast with Lydia. She was relieved that Lydia had long ago insisted that she would take care of the usual chores and preparing their breakfast on Sunday mornings. She took a minute to steady her breathing as she felt the flush of exertion from having run all the way back after leaving the note for Luke. She hoped she could trust the man.

Trust.

Perhaps Josef had looked to the future and seen a lifetime of uncertainty when it came to trusting her. For it was true — as often as he had declared his love for her, she had never once been able to bring herself to say the words to him. She had simply accepted that she and Josef were meant for one another and she had believed with all her heart that in time she would come to love him as much as she liked him.

Her head reeled with the need to find

some logical explanation for his sudden decision to quit her, and then to find an equally agreeable solution to this sudden upheaval. On a morning when she had expected to arrive at services and hear her name linked with Josef's in the announcement of coming nuptials, she must instead wonder how she could possibly endure the day. For endure it she must. Even if Luke found her note and showed up to drive them to services, chatter about a romance between Lydia and Luke would take time to develop. And there was always the possibility that Lydia would refuse to accept the ride.

And what of the added humiliation if Josef had failed to tell Bishop Troyer not to include them when he made the announcement?

"Liddy," she called out, her voice shaking with panic as she flung open the door of her bedroom. "Liddy!"

CHAPTER THREE

Lydia came running down the hall from the kitchen. "What is it? Are you all right?" Greta looked up at her sister with tear-filled eyes and an expression of pure panic. Lydia rushed to her side. "Come, sit. Take a deep breath."

Greta did as her sister instructed. Since their mother's death when Greta was only a toddler, she had relied on Lydia to show her the way through the travails of daily life. "What if . . ." She drew in a long breath and gasped, "What if Josef has not spoken with Bishop Troyer? What if . . ."

Lydia frowned, a sure sign that she had not considered this possibility and was even now working through the logistics of how best to handle this latest crisis in Greta's life. "Well, we shall simply have to make certain that the bishop knows what has happened. Therefore, it would be best if we arrived at services as soon as possible."

Greta nodded. "You'll speak with him?"

"Bishop Troyer? Of course, but Greta, he is likely to want to speak with you — and Josef."

Greta groaned.

"Now, sister, it's not necessarily as dire as you may think. As I told you last night," Lydia continued, "I suspect that Josef has simply had a bout of nerves. Marriage is a big step. There is every possibility that after a night's lost sleep he regrets his impulsive action and has not yet figured out how to set things right again."

When Greta had told Lydia the news over supper the evening before, she had taken great comfort and hope from her sister's reassurances. But Lydia might know many things — might even be the smartest person in all of Celery Fields — still when it came to matters of the heart, Lydia had almost no experience and besides, didn't Greta know Josef better than anyone did? Although he had a reputation for being wishy-washy, once he did settle on a plan of action, he could be as stubborn as any other man when it came to changing his mind.

And yet when she heard the snort of a horse and the soft plodding of hooves on the sandy road that ran past their house and on out to the countryside, Greta flew to the window. She could not help but hope that it would be Josef bringing his buggy to collect the two sisters for services as he had done ever since their father had died a year earlier. In that instant she played out the entire scene of how he would come to the door, hat in hand, eyes on the ground. And she would greet him as if nothing had passed between them the day before. The three of them would climb into his buggy and arrive at services as they had every other Sunday.

But when she looked outside there was no buggy. Instead there was a wagon with a matched team of black Percheron horses and climbing down from the driver's seat was none other than the blacksmith, Luke Starns.

"What on earth?" Lydia had followed Greta to the window and was also watching Luke approach the house.

"He's come to drive us to services," Greta said. "He offered," she added with a shrug as Lydia's eyebrows lifted in surprise.

"And you accepted this offer of a ride with a man we barely know?" Lydia asked, her voice the one she used when questioning a student.

"Not right away," Greta stammered. "I mean I thought about it and well, Josef is certainly not going to call for us."

There was a knock at the door. It was five minutes before eight o'clock. "I told him to come at eight," Greta added.

"Come drink your tea and eat something," Lydia said with a resigned sigh. "I'll get the door."

Theirs was a small house and Greta did not really have to eavesdrop to overhear the exchange between Lydia and the blacksmith. She nibbled at a slice of rye bread as her sister greeted Luke.

"You are early, Luke Starns. My sister is just having her breakfast."

Greta frowned. "Oh, Liddy," she whispered to herself. "Show the man a little kindness."

She heard Luke mumble an apology.

"Well, come in out of the heat," Lydia instructed.

While Lydia marched down the hallway to the kitchen, Greta saw that Luke had remained uncertainly by the front door.

"Liddy," Greta hissed, "offer the man some juice."

"We do not have time for juice, Greta." She took a cloth napkin and wiped a crumb from the corner of Greta's mouth. "Now, come along or we'll be late."

Outside, Lydia stood aside, making it clear

that she expected Greta to climb up to the wagon's only seat first. "It's going to be another hot day," Greta said, trying to ease the tension that hung over the trio as heavily as the humidity. "Even for August," she added when they were all three seated.

But it was apparent that she could not expect comments from either Lydia or Luke. Both of them were sitting as if someone had placed a board against their backs and they were each staring straight ahead, their mouths tightly set into thin lines. Clearly any attempt Greta might make to start a conversation was useless so she bowed her head and folded her hands in her lap. She might as well put the time to good use — praying that somehow she might get through this day.

At Pleasant's house, where services were to be held, Pleasant's husband, Jeremiah, came forward to welcome them. If he thought it odd that they should arrive with Luke Starns, he gave no sign.

"Is your great uncle inside, Jeremiah?" Lydia asked as he helped her down from the wagon. Jeremiah's uncle was the head of their congregation.

"Yes. Is there a problem? Has something happened?" He was clearly mystified that Lydia's first comment would be to ask the whereabouts of the congregation's bishop without so much as a greeting for him. Greta felt a touch of relief as she realized that at least Jeremiah seemed to have no idea at all that Josef had quit her.

"Greta just needs to ask him a question," Lydia replied with a smile. She waited for Jeremiah to help Greta down then turned to Luke. "Thank you, Luke Starns, for the ride. My sister and I will be staying to help Pleasant prepare the barn for tonight's singing and can find our way home after that."

In spite of her own worries, Greta rolled her eyes heavenward as if seeking God's help. No wonder Lydia had never had a serious beau. She treated every man she met as if he were one of her students. She saw that Luke had been about to say something to Lydia, then thought better of it.

"Are you better?" Greta heard Luke murmur and realized that he was addressing her while Lydia was already halfway across the yard on her way to the large farmhouse.

"I am perfectly fine, Luke." She offered him a tight smile. "And having kept my end of our bargain I trust that . . ."

"I'm not given to gossip, Greta, but you should prepare yourself because soon enough . . ."

"Greta." Lydia was expert at delivering an

entire lecture with a single word. In two syllables she had effectively reminded Greta that it was the Sabbath, that they were to turn their hearts and minds to God and that the bishop was no doubt awaiting her arrival.

As the two sisters walked toward the house, Greta glanced back over her shoulder toward the barn where Luke was now unhitching the horses while Jeremiah greeted more neighbors. Luke was right, of course. It hardly mattered what he might have said to Roger Hadwell. By the end of today's service everyone would know.

"Let's get this over with," she said as she and Lydia reached the front door of Pleasant's home.

Inside the modest white frame house, the backless wooden benches, transported from house to house for the biweekly services, had been set up in the two large front rooms that were a feature of every Amish home. From down the hall that led to the kitchen, Greta could hear the voices of those women and girls who had already arrived. They would gather there to deliver their contributions for the light meal that would follow the three-hour service. She and Lydia were each carrying a basket that held their contributions for the meal. It was a comfort to realize that the women all seemed to be talking in a normal tone, not whispering as she might have expected.

Pleasant rushed forward to greet them.

"Could you take these?" Lydia asked, handing Pleasant her basket. "Greta needs to speak with Bishop Troyer."

"Of course," Pleasant replied, taking Greta's basket, as well. "Something to do with a certain announcement to be made today?" she asked and she actually winked.

Greta forced a smile as Lydia took her arm. "We won't be long," she assured Pleasant.

"Maybe it would be better if we just told everyone now," Greta murmured. "At least then it would be out in the open." On the other hand, there was still time for Josef to find her, tell her he'd been wrong, beg her forgiveness.

They passed through the front hall separating the rooms where services would be held. They dodged a group of small children racing up the stairs. The younger men and boys tended to linger outside until others took their places for the service.

Glancing around for any sign of Josef, Greta turned toward the hallway that led to a downstairs bedroom, knowing the bishop and other elders always gathered there before the services began. She was about to tell Lydia to go to the kitchen when she practically ran into Josef. Through the open doorway behind him, she could see Bishop Troyer and the two other preachers who would speak that morning. They were all looking at her, their eyes full of pity.

"*Guten morgen,* Josef," she said brightly as she edged around him in the narrow hallway.

"I have just told them," Josef said without returning her greeting or meeting her eyes.

"*Gut,*" Greta murmured with no further pretense at acting as if anything about this morning was normal.

"Greta?" Bishop Troyer had come to the doorway. "I wonder if I might have a word with you and Josef before services begin?" The other church elders left the room and Bishop Troyer closed the door.

Woodenly Greta sat down on the only chair in the room. Normally she would have remained standing out of respect but the truth was that, upon seeing Josef, her knees had gone weak and she wasn't at all sure that she could maintain her balance without support. Josef stayed close by the door, studying the wide planks of the wooden floor.

"Josef has told me of your decision," he began.

Her decision?

She glanced up at Josef and saw that his cheeks had gone red. "It was my decision, Bishop," he muttered. "Greta . . ." He shrugged which only infuriated her more.

Greta what? Had no say in the matter?

Bishop Troyer seemed momentarily perplexed. "I see," he murmured. "When you told me that you and Greta would not be marrying this autumn, I just assumed that . . ."

"It was my decision," Josef repeated.

"The fact is, Bishop, that we won't be marrying at all," Greta added, surprised to hear the words come out of her mouth.

Josef looked up then, his eyes wide with shock. "Well, that is . . ."

"Isn't that what you told me?" she challenged. She stood up and realized that her anger at the unfairness of the situation had given her strength. "It's for the best, don't you think?" This she directed to the bishop.

The kindly white-haired man who had been the head of their church for as long as Greta could remember looked at her and then at Josef, his brow furrowed with concern. "This is a time for prayer — not haste. You must both ask God to show you His

58

plan for your lives. It is true that you and others have long assumed that His intention was for the two of you to share a life. And that may yet be the way of it. This is not for either of you to decide without first praying on the matter."

"It was not a decision made in haste," Josef replied.

"Then why?" Greta blurted out before the bishop could speak. "Is there someone else?"

Josef looked at her and she saw for the first time the pain that lined his features. "How many times have I asked you that question," he said softly. "I have asked it time and again."

"And time and again I have told you that you are imagining things."

"And yet, not once have you said that you love me, Greta."

It was true and there were no words to deny it. Fortunately she was saved by a soft knock on the door. "Pastor?" she heard one of the other ministers say. "It's time."

Josef opened the door and brushed past the two other preachers waiting in the hallway.

"Come along, child," the bishop said as he led the way down the hall and into the front room where Josef had already taken his seat with the other men. Greta took her place next to Lydia on the first of two benches where the unmarried girls and women were seated.

In spite of the cool reception he'd received from Lydia that morning, Luke was determined to ask to see her home later that evening. If she refused him at least he would know where he stood. It would have complex ramifications, for if Lydia Goodloe turned him down, he might have to think seriously about moving on to another community. But one step at a time. Having settled on his plan, he was free to focus all of his attention on the words of Bishop Troyer — a lesson that seemed directed at him. But, of course, that wasn't possible. He'd taken care to keep his past to himself since his arrival in Celery Fields. But the flicker of panic he felt whenever he thought there was the possibility of others learning of his past was never far from the surface of his emotions.

The lesson came from the twenty-ninth chapter of the book of Genesis. It was the story of Jacob's love for Rachel and how her father, Laban, tricked Jacob into marrying his elder daughter, Leah, instead. Two sisters, the elder less desirable than the younger. And although the minister's sermon was about Laban's deceit, all Luke could think about was the biblical sisters. In the end Jacob had married them both but God had given him children by Leah while the much beloved Rachel remained barren. Had that been God's punishment? And if so, why punish a man like Jacob who had worked years for the privilege of marrying the woman he truly loved?

Luke shifted uncomfortably on the hard wooden bench as he remembered another pair of sisters — this time in Ontario. Their father had also been anxious to see his eldest daughter married and he had set his sights on Luke as the best possible candidate. But Luke was drawn to the man's younger, fairer daughter just as Jacob had been. And just like Jacob the father had tried to trick him into the match with the elder daughter. Only Luke — unlike Jacob — had refused to be drawn into such a plot.

When everything had turned out for the worst, Luke had often wondered if God had punished him for his refusal to even consider courting, much less marrying the older sister. But in that Biblical world multiple wives were allowed — Jacob could marry Leah and the beloved Rachel, as well. Luke did not have that choice. In the end his only real choice had been to leave the community where he had lived his whole life and move to a place where he could start over. Celery Fields had seemed the perfect place.

He glanced over to the bench where Lydia Goodloe sat, her eyes riveted on the pastor, her hands folded piously in her lap, her face intent as she took in the lesson of the sermon. Luke did not love her — how could he? He barely knew her other than to nod politely whenever they crossed paths. Still he had observed that she was a good and steadfast woman. In spite of her strictness, the children who were her students clearly admired her. Yes, Lydia Goodloe would be a wise choice to manage his home and raise his children in the faith of their ancestors. He could do a lot worse than Lydia Goodloe.

But then his gaze was drawn to the sister — Greta. Unlike Lydia, Greta's eyes did not remain fixed on the minister. Instead, she glanced around, out the window, up at the ceiling, at some lint she picked off her dark green cotton dress. Although she sat relatively still, her eyes darted around the room like a butterfly pausing at one flower and then quickly moving on to the next.

It occurred to Luke that if he were successful in his courtship of the elder sister, he would no doubt be expected to take in the younger one, as well. In the absence of her late parents, he and Lydia would be Greta's guardians, at least until she married. He could only pray that Josef Bontrager would reconsider his decision and take Greta for his wife.

Just then Greta's eyes lighted on him for an instant and he saw her scowl before quickly ducking her head and folding her hands in her lap. Likewise, Luke turned his attention back to the minister. As the words of the lesson continued, Luke silently prayed for God's guidance for this treacherous trip he was about to take down the path of courtship. At least this time he had chosen the elder sister with his eyes wide open. In this case there was no father to trick him as Laban had tricked Jacob or the man in Ontario had tried to deceive Luke.

No. The challenge facing him was to persuade Lydia Goodloe that they could make a nice life together. Convinced that he was up to that challenge, he risked one more look across the aisle at the Goodloe sisters and was unnerved when he realized that his gaze had settled first on Greta before moving on to Lydia.

Chapter Four

Greta squeezed her eyes shut tightly as the service came to an end, praying that God might forgive her for not listening to the lesson for the day. Oh, she had gotten the part about two sisters — one fairer than the other — but then her mind had started to wander. Surely the Lord would understand that she had so many things to consider — so many things to work out. The worst of it would be how best to handle the barely perceptible murmur that would surely spread through the congregation after Bishop Troyer announced the couples planning to marry that fall. That list, of course, no longer included Josef and her. So, soon everyone would know at least a part of the story. She brightened a little as it occurred to her that, like the bishop, most would simply assume that Greta had quit Josef rather than the other way round. Their pity would be directed toward him.

But then her relief collapsed as she realized that this was only a momentary reprieve. Soon enough everyone would know the real story. She glanced over toward the men's section, meaning to see how Josef was handling things but her eyes had settled instead on Luke Starns. The man was watching her and the only way she could describe his expression was one of disapproval. At that very moment, Lydia nudged Greta with her elbow — her signal for Greta to stop fidgeting. Those two were going to make a perfect match, she thought, as she laced her fingers together in silent prayer. It would appear that Luke Starns followed the rules as strictly as her sister.

The announcement of coming nuptials was made and the congregation reacted exactly as Greta had imagined. When the service finally ended, the women moved as one toward the kitchen to lay out the meal while the men and boys began rearranging the benches into tables and seating. She heard Josef's laugh and whipped around to see him stepping aside to allow Esther Yoder to pass by on her way to the kitchen.

Esther was the eldest daughter of the Yoders who owned the dry goods store. She was two years younger than Greta and it was well-known throughout Celery Fields that her mother thought it high time she found herself a husband. From the looks of things she had set her sights on Josef.

Well, she can have him, Greta thought swallowing her bitterness even as Lydia took hold of her elbow and turned her away from the scene.

"Come along, sister."

On their way to the kitchen they crossed paths with Luke, one long black bench under each powerful arm. He looked from Lydia to Greta and then back again. To Greta he seemed rooted to the spot like the giant live oak tree that stood outside his shop and she couldn't help but smile at the ridiculous comparison.

He cleared his throat. "May I speak with you later, Lydia Goodloe?"

Greta thought she had never seen her sister quite so shaken. Her lips were pressed together so tightly that no sound could possibly be expected to come out, so Greta took matters into her own hands.

"We are needed in the kitchen. But if you plan to attend the singing, then there will be time enough to have your say. Excuse us, *bitte.*"

Luke stepped aside and this time it was Greta who guided her sister the rest of the way to the kitchen.

"How could you say such a thing?" Lydia whispered when she had recovered her voice. "I had thought you of all people would wish to skip this evening's singing."

"Of course we must attend the singing, Lydia. Luke Starns wishes to see you home afterward. Will you accept or not?"

Lydia's eyes widened in disbelief. "How do you know such a thing?"

"He told me so."

Further conversation was not possible as they joined the other women in the kitchen. As Greta had feared, the room went silent the minute that she and Lydia entered.

Greta saw her choice plainly — she could pretend that nothing was out of the ordinary or she could address the matter and get it over with. She took stock of the glances flying among the women — lifted eyebrows of speculation and worried frowns of curiosity.

"Well," she said brightly as she picked up the baskets that she and Lydia had brought and began setting out the goods. "It sounds like we're going to have a busy season of weddings here in Celery Fields." She grinned broadly at the three other women whose betrothals had been announced that morning. "Perhaps it's a good thing Josef Bontrager changed his mind about marrying me."

She couldn't help it. Her voice broke on those last words, but she kept her tears in check and continued to place the food from the basket on the table.

Almost as one unit, the women gathered around her. She felt consoling hands placed gently on her shoulder and gratefully accepted the healing power of their murmurs of concern, which comforted her like a soothing balm for her jumbled spirit.

"Perhaps the Lord has another plan for you, Greta," Pleasant said softly. "We sometimes think we know what He has in store for us but then things change."

Of all people, Pleasant knew what she was talking about. Certainly she had thought she would never marry and then she had agreed to marry the widower, Merle Obermeier. He had died soon after, leaving her penniless with his four children from his first marriage to raise. And then Jeremiah Troyer, the bishop's great-nephew, had moved to town, just as the depression was starting, to open — of all things — an ice cream shop.

But the likelihood of some stranger moving into town and making everything all right again for Greta seemed remote at best. With the combination of droughts and deluges that had plagued the fields of celery and other produce crops over the last few seasons, people were beginning to move away from Celery Fields — not settle there. The last person to actually come to town had been Luke Starns.

Luke Starns . . . and Lydia.

Suddenly Greta saw her opportunity to turn the attention of the women away from her and on to something that would give them far greater pleasure. "You are right, Pleasant. After all, who knows what the Lord has in store for any of us when it comes to matters of the heart." She cast a sideways glance at Lydia, leading the other women to do the same.

As usual Hilda Yoder took charge. "I noticed that the two of you arrived for services with the blacksmith, Luke Starns. Has your horse pulled up lame, Lydia?"

"The blacksmith was kind enough to offer us a ride," Lydia replied as she sliced a loaf of bread.

"Roger tells me that he will definitely be settling here permanently. His business is doing surprisingly well given the fact that there's less call for services like his these days," Gertrude Hadwell, wife of the hardware store owner, said with a sly glance at Lydia. "It's hardly any secret, Lydia, that he has his eye on you."

"Then offering you a ride was the first step," Hilda announced.

"Toward what?" Lydia asked, her cheeks turning a deeper shake of pink than usual.

"Toward courtship, of course. I expect that he'll ask to see you home after tonight's singing? It's no one's business, of course. Such matters are private, but still . . ."

Lydia lifted her chin, hoisted the platter stacked high with sliced bread and said, "He will have to work up his nerve first, but if he asks I will accept."

Greta was every bit as shocked by this announcement as any of the women in the kitchen. Lydia had always said that she could not be bothered with courtship unless she were truly in love. She barely knew Luke Starns so what could she be thinking?

Luke filled his plate but kept his eyes on Lydia Goodloe. The truth was that the schoolteacher intimidated him the same way his former teacher had back in Ontario. How on earth was he going to court this woman? Where would he find the words? And why did the mere intent to do so feel more like a difficult task — one he would rather not attend — than something that would lead to a pleasant conclusion?

Perhaps the best plan was to approach her

with the idea that a match between them was a practical decision. He wanted a family. Her job as teacher of the community's children might be in jeopardy if families kept leaving Celery Fields to return north. How would she and her sister make their way if she lost her position? Would it not be a relief for her to surrender the burden of trying to make ends meet?

The more Luke thought about it, the more it seemed to him that this could work out to the mutual benefit of both parties. And grasping that, his confidence grew. At least until he spotted Greta. She presented a problem. The idea of living in a house with two women was not especially appealing. The idea of living there with the capricious Greta Goodloe was unnerving altogether. Of course Greta might yet marry. But who?

Unless Josef Bontrager changed his mind, who was there?

"Would you like some pie, Luke?"

Lydia was standing next to him. She was smiling although somehow her smile did not seem to quite reach her eyes. In her expression he read something else — something more like resignation.

"Denki." He took the plate and fork. "Did you make this?"

"I did."

Luke speared a bite of the pie and ate it. Without a doubt it was the worst-tasting peach pie he'd ever had. The fruit was hard and undercooked and had none of the enhancement of cinnamon or sugar to help flavor it and the crust was doughy and heavy. He swallowed the lumpy mess and smiled. *"Denki,"* he said again, unwilling to tell a lie especially on the Sabbath.

To his surprise Lydia burst out laughing. "It's horrid, I know." She relieved him of the plate and replaced it with another that she picked up from the spread of desserts on the table. "Try this one. Greta and my half sister, Pleasant, are the bakers in our family. I thought you might want to know that if indeed you are intent on . . . spending time with me."

And there before him was the opportunity he'd been seeking. In fact it appeared he did not even need to ask — although it would be rude and conceited not to. And the truth was that when she smiled, Lydia Goodloe was not quite so intimidating.

"I will be at tonight's singing," he began. "I understand that you — and your sister — will also be there?"

"We will indeed." Greta Goodloe stepped up next to them, her eyes twinkling mischievously.

Luke swallowed around the lump that seemed to be blocking his ability to speak. *"Das ist gut,"* he murmured and speared another bite of the pie.

"My sister will need a ride home," Greta prompted.

"We both will," Lydia corrected.

Luke had not counted on seeing the two of them home. That was hardly the way things were done. "I would be pleased to drive you — both."

"Then in that case," Lydia said, "we will see you this evening."

Luke watched the two of them move through the gathering, clearing plates and glasses as they went. Within minutes they had both gone back inside the farmhouse where the women would finish packing up the leftover food while the men moved the benches into the barn for the singing. He turned to help with the benches and found himself working next to Josef.

Luke had not liked Bontrager from the day he'd first come into the blacksmith's shop to hire Luke to check the team of giant Belgian horses he used to plow his fields. The man had instantly reminded Luke of the milk toast his father used to make for him and his brothers — soggy. It was an odd word to use in describing

73

another man, but it fit Josef Bontrager as far as Luke was concerned.

For all his booming voice, Josef was timid and indecisive when it came to business. And to Luke's way of thinking, he was penny-wise but pound-foolish as the old saying went. On the one hand he had bought up the land of surrounding farms when those farmers had hit hard times and decided to return to their homes up north. On the other he was dickering over paying the price for a proper shoe for his horse. When Luke had told him that three of the team of four horses would need at least one shoe replaced, Josef had hedged.

"You're certain we couldn't get by one more season?"

Luke had shrugged. "In my opinion you'd be taking a risk but it's your team."

Josef multiplied what Luke had given him as the price for one shoe times the total number that he recommended replacing. He tapped the stubby pencil against the final tally for a long moment and then released a low whistle through his teeth. "That's pretty steep," he said.

"That's my price," Luke replied as he packed up his equipment and climbed onto his horse. "Let me know if you decide to go ahead."

A full two weeks later — after Josef, according to Roger, had gotten at least two other bids — the farmer came to the shop and hired Luke to do the work. By that time all four horses were in need of his wares. And when Josef had hinted that Luke was simply trying to get more money for his work, Luke had told him the price he'd originally quoted would stand. He did this not for the owner, but out of pity for the horse. No, Luke did not much care for Josef Bontrager. And the more he saw of Greta Goodloe, the more he had to wonder what she had ever seen in the man.

Greta felt immeasurably better as she and Lydia worked together later that afternoon laying out the "thin book" version of the centuries-old Amish hymnal, the Ausband. The full version of the hymnal was used for regular services. It was thick — well over five hundred pages and contained the words of hymns passed down through the generations as far back as anyone could remember. The book contained no musical notations — just words. Because most of the hymns had been written during the time of persecution in Europe when Joseph Amman had broken from the Mennonites but not from the Anabaptist beliefs, the hymns they sang during services tended to be somber and even mournful in tone. By contrast the "thin book" version of the Ausband contained hymns that were lighter and more joyful and far more suitable for the kind of social occasion that the Sunday night singing was.

Greta was actually beginning to look forward to the evening. Her plan appeared to have worked. Instead of everyone buzzing about Josef's breakup with her, they were speculating about what Lydia had been thinking offering Luke Starns that piece of pie and what might the two of them have had to discuss for such an extended time. Just wait until Lydia left with Luke after the singing.

"The blacksmith seems nice," she ventured.

"Hmm." Lydia was noncommittal as always.

"He's very strong. Did you see the way he lifted two benches at once as if they were no more than small branches?"

"He's a blacksmith," Lydia pointed out. "In his line of work one develops strength."

Greta gauged her sister's mood. She seemed indifferent to the conversation, focusing instead on the precise alignment of each songbook. Every now and then she would reach across the long table and straighten a book that Greta had set in place before moving on.

"Still, he's quite handsome. I mean in a dark, brooding sort of way. Do you think perhaps that's the way men are in Ontario?"

"Ontario?" Lydia blinked at her as if she'd heard that single word and nothing else.

"Where he's from," Greta reminded her. "Canada?"

"I know where Ontario is," Lydia replied. "And I know what you are trying to do, Greta."

Greta bit her lip. "I'm just . . ."

". . . trying to take the attention of others away from your current troubles. And that is understandable. Furthermore I am quite willing to help you in that, but do not for one minute think that I am the least bit interested in Luke Starns — at least romantically speaking."

"You don't even know the man," Greta protested. "For all you know he might be . . ."

"I am sure that he is a good and kind man. From what I have heard from others, he is honest and fair in his business dealings and he seems quite determined to make a life for himself here in Celery Fields. The question I have is why?"

"Why does anyone come here? The

77

weather for one thing. I mean, Ontario?" Greta shivered in spite of the oppression of the heat.

"But alone — no family ties here? At least when Jeremiah Troyer arrived he had connections — his great-uncle and aunt were here and he had visited them in the past."

Greta sighed happily. "Yes, and then Jeremiah set his sights on Pleasant and it was so romantic."

"You're missing the point, Greta. Luke Starns simply . . ." She seemed lost for the right word. "He simply appeared one day. No one knew him or anything about him for that matter." They had finished their task and as Lydia surveyed their work she added, "And once again you are losing sight of the point of our conversation."

"Which is?"

"Which is, dear sister, that I am going to attend the singing tonight and allow Luke to see us home because it will indeed give people something to talk about other than you and Josef. However, get one thing straight." She pointed her forefinger at Greta the way she often pointed it at students in her classroom. "After tonight you will need to face the fact that there will be gossip and speculation regarding you and Josef and your best path is to ignore it and move forward."

Greta blinked back tears. "With what?"

"Pardon?"

"Move forward with what, Lydia?" Greta snapped peevishly. "You have your teaching. Even before she met Jeremiah, Pleasant had the bakery and the children. What exactly do I have to move forward with?"

And just like that, the misery returned, the misery she had felt once she realized that Josef was not going to come running back to her, not going to beg for her forgiveness, not going to — marry her. "I gave that man all my time — every waking hour was spent thinking about him, what would most please him and now . . ."

"Do not exaggerate, sister. You have our house to oversee — the cleaning and cooking, the laundry, the upkeep," Lydia scolded. "You and Josef spent a great deal of time together. That's true. Often, I might add, to the neglect of your responsibilities. Our house has not had a good cleaning in months. I think you will find that, if you keep yourself busy and away from the shops, in time you will find your way."

So she was to be a castaway, banished to the house until the talk died away? Greta whirled around to face her sister. "I keep up with the housework just fine. Papa used to say that it was the best-kept house in all of Celery Fields and that Josef was fortunate to have won the heart of one who . . ."

Lydia was fighting to hide a smile — and failing. "Feeling a little better?" she asked.

It was an old pattern the sisters had established early in their motherless lives — whenever Greta felt sorry for herself, Lydia would turn the tables on her. She would find some fault with Greta, knowing that the criticism would not go unchallenged.

"Yah," Greta admitted. *"Aber . . ."*

Lydia shushed her. "It's the Sabbath, Greta. Time for us to gather our thoughts and ruminate on the week past and the week to come." As was her habit on Sunday afternoons, Lydia retrieved the Bible she carried with her and walked outside where she sat on a bench under the shade of a tree and began to read.

Greta knew that her sister would spend hours reading scripture and praying before the cold supper they would share with Pleasant and her family. Ever since their father's death a year earlier, Lydia had isolated herself this way on Sunday afternoons. At first Greta had been hurt by what she saw as her sister's abandonment and had roamed the rooms of the house until it was time for Josef to come by so they could

80

go out walking or for a ride in his buggy. But then Lydia had explained that it was Greta's restlessness that had driven her to seek the refuge of her reading.

"You are in constant motion and I need the quiet," she had said. "We each have our way."

It was true. Greta did her best thinking — and praying — on her feet. Sometimes — like today — she would go for a walk. Fallow fields that had once provided enough to support the farmers stretched out as far as she could see. Here and there, those neglected fields were interrupted by a span of freshly plowed and planted fields — land that would yield crops to support the families remaining in the community. She turned her gaze to the distant silo that stood next to the large barn on Josef's farm, marking the otherwise undisturbed horizon. On other Sundays she had waited for him to join her. But not this Sunday . . . or next . . . or the ones beyond that. . . . She turned away from anything that might remind her of Josef. How could he have been so cruel?

A motion outside the barn caught her eye. Luke Starns was taking something from the back of his wagon. Greta frowned. The man ought to have a proper buggy for courting her sister. She glanced to where Lydia sat reading and trying to catch whatever breeze there might be. She doubted that Lydia would care one way or the other about a buggy, but Greta cared for her. Maybe they did things differently in Canada. Greta folded her arms in her apron and continued watching the blacksmith — who seemed totally oblivious to her presence.

He took off the jacket he'd worn during services and placed it on the wagon seat. Then he pushed back the sleeves of his shirt and led one of his team of horses into Jeremiah's barn before returning for the other. As he went about these tasks she could see his suspenders stretch over the muscles of his broad back. She couldn't help thinking that in spite of the years farming and building furniture for the Yoders to sell in their store, Josef was given to the pudginess that had plagued him as a boy.

"Too fond of Pleasant's pies," he had often teased, patting his oversize stomach. And certainly he was a regular customer at the bakery. Since most of his family had moved north again, he lived alone and at least twice a week he was at the bakery buying a couple dozen of the large glazed doughnuts that were Pleasant's specialty and always a pie — sometimes two.

Greta felt her cheeks flush at the realization that she was actually comparing Josef's physical appearance to Luke's. What was the matter with her? She forced herself to turn away. She needed to concentrate on how best to get Lydia to allow the blacksmith to court her. Her sister could be so stubborn sometimes.

After he'd finished helping Jeremiah and the other men set up the benches for the evening singing, Luke had intended to head to town. But the truth was that once there he'd have little more than an hour before he'd just have to turn around and come back again. And in this heat even if he washed himself and groomed the horses in town, he and his team were bound to be sweat-soaked and dust-covered by the time he returned. No, best to stay here.

Jeremiah wouldn't mind and it would give Luke the time he needed to sort things out properly in his mind. Things that yesterday had seemed fairly straightforward now made little sense. His decision to persuade the schoolteacher that they would make a good match had seemed so simple in theory. In other parts of the country, there were several Amish communities within several miles of each other allowing for a much broader opportunity to get to know others.

But in Celery Fields there were no outlying or neighboring Amish communities and so there were few options for single men and women.

The idea that Lydia might rebuff him had never even entered his thinking. Yet he'd had the distinct feeling earlier that she had agreed to be seen leaving the singing with him tonight for one reason only — to turn the attention of the gossips away from Greta and onto her. On the one hand he admired her loyalty to her sister. On the other the realization that Lydia found such a drastic move necessary only served to remind him that Greta was no longer a detail that he could overlook as he considered the future.

In the time he had spent considering how best to pursue Lydia as his wife, he had never given much thought to Greta. Like everyone else in town, he had assumed she would marry Josef and that would be the end of it. But now . . .

Now he found himself thinking about how the house he had thought to share with Lydia would also be home to Greta — at least unless Bontrager came to his senses or some other man in the community stepped up to court her. He and both Goodloe sisters would share meals and holidays and outings. She would be there when he came home in the evenings and when he left for his shop in the mornings. It was enough to try and imagine himself settling in with one woman. Two — especially when one of them was the mercurial Greta — was more than he had bargained for. But it was too late to rethink his plan. In a matter of hours the singing would be over and he and the Goodloe sisters would be riding back to town — together — in the dark.

Greta represented a fly in the ointment of his plan. Yet he could not deny that earlier on their way to services, he had been uncomfortably aware of Greta's closeness, positioned as she was between him and Lydia on the high wagon seat. Her shoulder had been only a fraction of an inch from his upper arm. When he had tried to steal a glance at Lydia to see how she might be reacting to the clearly unexpected circumstances of riding to services with him, he had instead found himself looking at Greta — her fair ivory cheek and full pink lips just visible beneath the brim of her bonnet.

Yes, he had a problem. It was obvious to him that Lydia's first and primary concern was going to be caring for her sister. Any interest she might have in him was going to be a distant second. It was also obvious to him that he was spending far too much of his time thinking about Greta Goodloe.

Sometimes Greta loved the fact that Celery Fields was such a small, close-knit community. But as young people began to arrive for the evening singing, she would have happily traded her surroundings for a bustling, impersonal city. The singing was a far livelier occasion than Sunday services. Everyone mixed together, talking and laughing and sharing refreshments. Along with barn raisings, festivals and other community events, this was an approved venue for courtship and for flirtation.

She had been naive to imagine that everyone would be focusing on Luke and Lydia. After all, the idea of a courtship between her sister and the blacksmith was something townspeople had speculated on almost from the moment Luke Starns had arrived in Celery Fields. It was old news whereas Greta's breakup with Josef was fresh fodder for the gossip mill. Everyone would be far more interested in where she — and Josef — might choose to sit.

"Staying for the singing is a terrible idea," she announced as she plopped down next to Lydia on the bench where her sister had spent the afternoon reading.

"But I thought . . ." Lydia studied her for

a long moment. "I see. You are afraid of what people will say about you — and Josef."

"I am not afraid," Greta protested. "It's just that it's so soon and . . ."

"If we leave then I cannot accept Luke Starns's offer of a ride home," Lydia reminded her.

"Of course you can. In fact it makes more sense than my tagging along. I'll just pretend . . ."

"No. Either you and I both go home now or we both stay."

Greta could be every bit as stubborn as her sister. She folded her arms across her chest and said, "Then I guess we both go home. We can walk."

"Fine. You will go and tell Luke Starns of the change in plans," Lydia instructed. "Now."

"You should be the one. It's you he wants to see later," Greta argued.

"It was your decision to accept his offer to drive us here for services and it is now your decision to leave before the singing. You owe the blacksmith an explanation — in person."

"Fine," Greta huffed. As the sister of the woman that Luke intended to court, there was no reason for Greta not to be seen talking to Luke. Anyone observing them would assume that she was simply furthering the courtship on her sister's behalf. So Greta made no attempt to hide her destination as she stomped across the yard toward the barn. From inside the barn she could hear the snort of a horse and the deep, soft voice of Luke talking to the animal. She took a moment to close her eyes and pray for the right words and then she walked toward the stall at the far end of the barn.

"Luke Starns," she called out, inching her way forward as her eyes became accustomed to the shadows cast by a late afternoon sun.

He stepped out from the stall, holding a grooming brush in one hand. *"Yah?"*

Greta pasted a smile on her face although she doubted he could really see it. "I'm afraid that . . . That is my sister . . ."

Luke turned and continued brushing the horse. "Your sister is having second thoughts," he said flatly. It was not a question.

What it was though was a way out of this entire mess. If she agreed then there would be no further need for explanation. Greta chewed on her lip. But lying was a sin and that would definitely count as a lie.

"I am having second thoughts," she admitted.

The brush rested on the horse's hindquarters for a fraction of a second before Luke once again resumed the rhythmic stroking. "About me and your sister?"

"Oh no," she hurried to assure him. "Not at all."

"Then what?"

"Josef will be here for the singing." It was all the explanation she felt he needed. After all, he knew the whole story.

"*Yah.* And at least a dozen other people."

"All talking about us — Josef and me."

"That will happen whether or not you are here."

He was right, of course. "But . . ."

He continued grooming his horse. "It seems to me that this boondoggle is something like a wildfire. If you can contain it before it spreads too far then it'll die down a lot quicker."

The man was speaking in riddles. "And just how do you suggest I do that?"

He put down the brush and turned to face her. "Go to the singing tonight. Tomorrow go about your business — shopping, errands, whatever you would normally do. It's natural that you'd rather hole up in your house there until this thing burns itself out, but that'll take a lot longer than facing things head-on will."

The fact that she knew he was probably

right annoyed her. The fact that he thought she would "hole up in their house," when Greta Goodloe had not once in her life backed down from anyone, was just plain insulting. She drew herself up to her full height — a good six inches less than his — and took a step closer to him.

"You don't know the first thing about me, Luke Starns," she challenged and to her fury the man actually chuckled.

"You've got me there. But it seems to me that if you're in favor of us becoming family one day, then it might be a good idea for you and your sister and me to get better acquainted." He went back to brushing the horse. "So what's it going to be, Greta?"

He was daring her and clearly he thought she would not take the dare. Well, she would show him. She would show all of them. "My sister and I will be sitting at the far end of the table. Try to be there in time to take the seat across from her although I suspect most everyone will make sure you have that privilege," she announced and turned on her heel and marched out into the fading sunlight. Behind her she was sure that she heard Luke chuckling again.

CHAPTER FIVE

As Greta had predicted, Josef was at the singing. He had taken a seat directly across from the storekeeper's daughter. And Esther Yoder was lapping up this unexpected attention like a cat at a bowl of fresh cream.

With a defiant lift of her chin, Greta turned the beam of her smile on young Caleb Harnischer and took the seat opposite the boy. Caleb looked alarmed and at the same time Lydia jerked her head in the direction of Pleasant's stepdaughter, Bettina Obermeier. The girl had been about to take the place that Greta occupied.

"Sorry," Greta murmured and slid away from Lydia, leaving the space between them free for Bettina. When she recovered from her embarrassment, she glanced up and saw that she was seated across from Cyrus Bontrager — Josef's bachelor uncle. The man was something of a legend in town and not for good reasons. Over his fifty-some years he had attempted to pursue just about every eligible young woman in Celery Fields with no success. When he looked across the table and saw Greta sitting there, his eyes lit up.

A smothered giggle from Esther Yoder told Greta that she was once again the center of attention. She cast about in desperation for some way to take back control of her situation.

"Aah, Caleb," she asked, turning her attention to the boy who was five years her junior, "how are things at the ice cream shop?" Her voice sounded shrill and nervous even to her own ears, and drew the attention of several people up and down the table, to her horror.

Caleb murmured something in reply but Greta was beyond hearing him. Close to tears from the exhaustion of a sleepless night and the strain of the day, she stood up. "Excuse me," she murmured and started for the door. But Luke stepped around the table at that moment and blocked her way. "Let me pass," she whispered hoarsely.

"No," he murmured back although he was smiling at her. "Stand your ground." It occurred to her that his smile was meant not for her but for the others. The man was covering for her. He had been on his way to take his place next to Caleb and across from

Lydia. He glanced at Caleb as if he had simply joined the conversation. "It's amazing that in spite of hard times people still need their treats, right, Caleb?"

The boy grinned at Luke, clearly flattered that this man would engage him in conversation. "We'll have a fresh batch of butter pecan next Saturday," Caleb said. "That's your favorite, right?"

"It is. Do you know everyone's favorite flavor?"

"Just the regulars," Caleb replied shyly.

"And Greta Goodloe? What's her favorite?"

"Chocolate with nuts."

Greta noticed that everyone else seemed to have fallen back into the normal routine of getting settled onto the benches and greeting their friends.

"And Lydia Goodloe's?" Luke asked as he took his seat across from Greta's sister.

Up and down the table conversation paused as those near enough to overhear nodded knowingly as if they knew they had been right all along in assuming that Luke and Lydia would be together.

"Strawberry," Lydia said and to Greta's amazement her sister gave Luke the most radiant smile. Then she opened her songbook and looked over her shoulder at Greta.

"They are about to begin, sister." She nodded toward the empty space next to Bettina and across from Cyrus. Reluctantly Greta took her seat.

The singing seemed as endless as the service that morning. Greta felt as if she were a prisoner in the large barn lit by a line of kerosene lanterns spaced along the table. She could hardly ignore the way that Josef would every once in a while glance at Esther over the top of his songbook and smile. And as the evening wore on, Greta realized that the smiles Josef and Esther were exchanging were far too familiar to be the start of something new. No, those smiles were the smiles of two people who shared a secret.

So there had been someone else, Greta fumed silently and she made no pretense at keeping up with the words the others were singing. A combination of jealousy and guilt overwhelmed her and this time she needed no excuse to leave the table. Without a word she stumbled toward the open doors of the barn and the sanctity of the darkness beyond. She felt all eyes follow her as she hurried away and once outside she gulped in the humid night air and fought against the tears that she simply refused to allow herself to shed.

Cry over Josef Bontrager after everything she had put up with all these years? His moods, his insistence that everything be done to his satisfaction, his constantly trying to change her — mold her into some ideal he held of the perfect wife and mother?

That was it, she realized. All the time that Josef had courted her, he had been trying to change her. He didn't love *her,* she realized. He loved her appearance — took sinful pride in being seen with such a pretty and popular woman. But how many times when he spoke of their future had he reminded her that, once they were married, she would need to temper her curiosity and natural instinct to speak her mind?

And truth be told she had thought she could change him, as well — once they were married. She had imagined that he would become less reserved and more outgoing. She had been certain that the children they would have would soften his strict demeanor. But now, as she walked a distance from the barn to the bench where Lydia had sat earlier, she had to admit that she had been wrong — as wrong about Josef as he had been about her. And in her heart she forgave him for the pain he had caused her and she prayed for God's forgiveness for her own selfishness. "But, heavenly

Father, I cannot understand what You have in mind for me."

The darkness gave her the advantage of seeing without being seen and so she studied the gathering in the barn even as she tried to make sense of what God's plan for her could possibly be. She saw Lydia glance anxiously toward the yard a couple times but knew that her sister would not come to find her. Doing so would just call more attention to the situation and Lydia was a little like Josef in that she did not like being noticed by others.

Calmer now, Greta took a moment to consider Luke Starns. She wondered if Lydia had noticed how truly handsome he was. He did not smile readily or often but on the rare occasions when he did, his full lips parted to reveal even, white teeth and just the hint of a dimple in his left cheek. He was broad shouldered and well muscled — the result, as Lydia had suggested, of the work he did. And he was tall. That was good because Lydia was also tall — with dark hair and thick lashes and a smile that she kept mostly to herself.

Greta supposed that they would make a good match — at least they made a handsome pair. But she had now come to realize that outward appearances were far less important than what intentions and secrets might be kept inside. Lydia was right. What did anyone truly know about Luke Starns after all? The man had appeared in town last spring and purchased the livery business from the previous owner who had decided to move back north. He had quickly earned a reputation for honesty and hard work and those two traits had been enough for most people in town to accept him without question. But who was he?

Greta frowned — all thoughts of Josef gone as she focused on the dark stranger who had set his sights on her sister. In the absence of their parents or any other close family beyond Pleasant, surely it was up to her to look out for Lydia's best interests. Before she would condone a match she wanted to make certain that this man was exactly who he presented himself to be. *And what was that?* she wondered and realized that neither she nor Lydia nor anyone else in town had the slightest idea.

The minute he'd seen Greta flee the crowded room, Luke's instinct had been to go after her. But, of course, that would raise eyebrows up and down the table and the last thing she needed right now was more gossip and speculation. He glanced over at

Lydia. She kept her eyes lowered but with an almost imperceptible shake of her head seemed to read his thoughts and let him know that it would not do to go after Greta.

Still, he could not seem to help but worry about her, imagining her out there in the dark, heartbroken. She had had a difficult time of things these last two days and his heart went out to her. Greta wasn't like her sister. Lydia was strong willed and pragmatic. And she had a deep abiding faith that whatever might happen, it was God's will and would become clear in due time. Greta did not appear to be quite so blind in her faith and Luke realized that this was a trait that the two of them shared.

He forced his attention back to the singing and the barrel-chested Josef Bontrager seated three men away from him. The man had his head thrown back and eyes tightly closed as he raised his high-pitched — and slightly off-key — tenor in song. It was almost as if he was determined to call attention to himself. Or was he simply trying to drown out the vision of Greta running from the room? Watching him, Luke found himself curling his hands into fists. He had never in his life wanted to strike another human being the way he wanted to strike Josef. He forced his breathing to calm and relaxed the tension in his hands. Was it reasonable for him to feel so protective of the Goodloe woman? If it had been Lydia his reaction might make sense, but Greta?

Of course, in the future, if his plan to court Lydia worked out, Greta would become his sister-in-law. She would be family. And as such his instinct to protect her — especially if she remained unwed — would be normal. It would even be expected. But the venom he was feeling toward his fellow man at the moment seemed anything but brotherly concern. He was about to close his eyes and seek God's forgiveness for his rambling thoughts when a movement outside the double barn doors caught his eye and he saw that Greta Goodloe was standing just out of the pool of light cast by the lanterns. Her arms were folded across her rigid body and if he didn't know better he would think that she was staring not at Bontrager — but at him.

With relief Greta heard the gathering launch into the final song of the evening. *Gott ist die Liebe* was everyone's favorite and seemed a fitting conclusion to a day that had begun with prayer and ended in song. Now everyone would spend the next half hour visiting and enjoying some refreshments before heading home.

In the past she and Josef had often been the center of a lively group of young people, talking and laughing before the two of them headed back to town in Josef's open-topped courting buggy. On such occasions Lydia would either have stayed home from the singing, staying the night with Pleasant or she would find her own way home to allow the courting couple their privacy. If Lydia went home, she would head to her room to pretend to sleep so that the couple could sit on the porch together. It struck Greta that tonight she would be the one to go off to her room and pretend sleep while Luke and Lydia sat together on the porch. Would Luke try to kiss Lydia? She found herself thinking about how his full, soft lips might feel.

"Stop that," she hissed, shocked at such a scandalous thought.

Once everyone had risen from the long table and gathered in small clusters near the entrance to the barn to partake of the refreshments that Pleasant had set out, it was easy to rejoin the group without making herself a spectacle. She slipped back into the gathering and took her place next to Lydia. Blessedly the others were more focused on the pastries and — in some cases

— each other as everyone enjoyed this rare opportunity to socialize. Greta nibbled at a cookie, nodding and smiling as the conversation swirled around her.

"Come help Pleasant carry these leftovers back to the house, Greta," Lydia instructed as she wiped the table with a damp cloth. "Then we should be getting home. It's been a long day and I have school tomorrow."

"Where's Luke?"

"I expect he's gone to hitch up his team," Lydia replied, handing Greta an empty platter and nodding toward the house.

Lydia's demeanor had not changed in the slightest. If she was nervous about Luke seeing her home she certainly didn't show it. *How does she do it?* Greta wondered as she carried the metal tray across the yard to the farmhouse. Nothing ever seemed to ruffle Lydia. Oh how Greta wished she could be as calm and serene as her sister was.

"Tell your sister that I have the wagon ready, Greta Goodloe."

The voice came out of the dark and startled her so much that she dropped the tray. When she bent to retrieve it, Luke was already there and their fingers brushed as he picked it up and handed it to her. "Sorry. I thought you saw me walking across the yard," he said. As the two of them slowly stood upright, Greta was far too aware of how very close their faces were. In the dim lamplight that glowed inside the kitchen and spilled out onto the back porch, she saw that he was studying her and his lips were parted in a half smile.

"What?" she demanded, touching her bonnet that must surely have been knocked askew.

"Nothing. You were looking right at me just before and yet it's as if you didn't see me at all." His voice softened as he added, "What had you so lost in thought that you didn't know I was here?"

"I was just . . . It's been a puzzling day."

"How so?"

She shot him a look as she clutched the empty tray to her chest. "Now you're making fun of me and that's just cruel, Luke Starns." She marched up the three porch steps but he was there ahead of her, holding open the screen door for her.

"Again I apologize. It's that for a moment back there you looked so . . ."

"So what?"

"Lost," he said.

The word mirrored her feelings and so overwhelmed her that she felt tears fill her eyes. "You should go and find my sister, Luke. I think I will stay the night here with

102

Pleasant and her family." The minute the words were out Greta knew that this was the best possible decision. She could help Pleasant with the children and her Monday chores and then walk back to town later tomorrow when everyone else would be occupied with their daily routines.

He frowned. "Don't make the mistake of hiding from your fears, Greta," he advised.

Greta laughed. "You are already beginning to sound like an older brother and you have not yet begun the first instance of courting my sister. Can you not see that I am doing you a favor? Now you will have my sister's company all to yourself."

Luke frowned and Greta sighed heavily. "Is this not what you want? My help in your courtship of my sister?"

"Your sister did not agree to be escorted home without you," he replied.

"Well, she will understand that my mind is made up and that she has no other choice but to accept your offer to take her home. Now go."

Greta did not think she had ever been as exhausted as she was in that moment. Honestly, was there no pleasing the male of the species?

Luke held the reins loosely in his right hand

as the team plodded along the familiar road. The night was pitch black without moon or stars and Lydia sat stone still beside him. So still that she might have been a piece of the wagon rather than a living, breathing human being. The two of them had not exchanged two words from the moment they had left the Troyers' farm. Even then her words had been for her sister, Greta, and for her half sister, Pleasant. Both of them had assured her that the idea of Greta staying the night was a blessing all around. But it was clear that Lydia remained unconvinced.

It was also evident that her concern was not about finding herself alone with him headed to a house where she would be alone for the night. In the Amish community courtship was a private matter — even among those as young as Caleb and Bettina. Routinely when a boy asked to see a girl home the parents would make it their business to be in bed, leaving the young couple the privacy of the porch where they could sit and talk and plan a future. In fact once a couple began seeing each other, it was assumed that both had already decided that the other had the necessary traits to make a good mate — patience, humility, frugality, hardworking and devoted to their faith.

Love did not enter into the decision for many. It was a practical decision — a next step in the routine of their earthly life. Luke had no reason not to believe that this would be the case between Lydia and him.

No. There would be no gossip about Lydia riding home alone with Luke tonight. Now if he had driven her home after services in broad daylight, that would be a different matter altogether. Once he and Lydia had begun their courtship it would be all right for Greta to ride with him in daylight, but not Lydia. Not until the bishop had announced their intention to wed.

Luke realized that he had allowed his thoughts to wander, unable to come up with any topic that might interest Lydia and lead to a conversation between them. They were almost halfway back to town when she cleared her throat and shifted slightly away from him on the wagon seat.

"We must discuss this, Luke," she announced as if they had been talking from the moment they left the farm.

"Bitte?"

"This business," she gritted out, flicking her forefinger back and forth between them. "This . . . courtship." The way she said the word it sounded as if it was something distasteful.

Luke bristled. He wasn't the smartest man in the community — certainly his book learning was nowhere near hers, but that did not mean that . . .

"We are too long past our youth to deceive ourselves, you and I," Lydia continued. "I admit that I do not fully know your reasons and I suppose that if we both set our minds to it we could have a satisfactory life together."

"But?" he prompted.

She actually turned toward him. "But why would either of us want such a life?"

"It is what we do, Lydia," he reminded her. "In our tradition we find a mate and if love comes then . . ."

"But why not marry for love in the first place?"

Luke was stunned. "That's just . . ." He fumbled for words.

"Not done?" She knotted her hands together in her lap. "Oh, but it is. In Celery Fields there have been two such instances just in the recent past — Hannah and Levi Harnischer were a most unlikely match. And Pleasant and Jeremiah? It seemed impossible and yet look at them. Look at the way they are with each other. Think how their love has brought such life and happiness to those dear children."

"Celery Fields is a small community, Lydia," he reminded her gently. "It's getting smaller each year as more people leave to return to homes and families up north. As you have already noted, you and I are no longer teenagers. If we are to have a marriage and children, then . . ."

"It sounds like a business arrangement," she huffed. "And I will have no part of it. I have a good life. I have my teaching and my students. I have no need of a union that is made for the sole purpose that it's the best we can manage."

Luke's hand tightened on the reins. He hardly knew what to say. Certainly he had misjudged this woman with her independent ideas and her sharp words that she seemed unaware could wound another person. "I may not be . . ." he began softly, then swallowed hard around the fury he was feeling and trying to control. "I would be a good provider, Lydia," he amended.

"Oh, Luke, forgive my thoughtless words. You are much respected throughout the community. But I am not blind, Luke. I saw the way you watched Greta tonight."

"Your sister . . ."

She interrupted his protest with a raised hand. "Actually I have observed you for some time now."

Luke looked over at her, surprised at this admission.

"Oh, don't look so shocked. It's common knowledge that all of Celery Fields has been planning a match for us. I needed to know exactly what such a match might offer."

"And I offer so little that you want to thrust me off onto your sister?"

"Now you are suffering from wounded pride. I love my sister, Luke. If I am saying that I see you as a good match for her then I am paying you the highest of praise. Rest assured that I never thought or said such a thing about Josef Bontrager."

"Which brings us to the heart of the matter," he argued. "Greta and Josef have been in love for . . ."

"My sister does not love that man — not in the way she needs to in order to spend the rest of her life under the same roof with him. Josef was a habit — a safe harbor in a community that offers women like my sister few choices. She has never loved him as more than a friend and surrogate brother."

"And what if he comes back to her, apologizes and . . ."

Lydia actually snorted with laughter. "Open your eyes, Luke. Did you not see the way he was flirting openly with Esther Yoder tonight?"

"Yes, but he could have been doing that just to make Greta jealous." Lydia's lack of a quick comment told him that she was considering this.

"Then there's no time to waste. Greta is most vulnerable at the moment." She turned to him. "It is evident that you are attracted to her, perhaps only now recognizing those feelings because of her break with Josef that makes her available for you to consider seriously."

"I have not once . . ."

"Please do not attempt to cover your feelings with excuses. I have long ago grown used to the fact that there is something about Greta that draws others to her — men and women and children alike. Why should you be any different?"

"I was going to say, your sister is someone who has a way about her, that's for sure. However, it was not your sister that I set my sights on when I decided to take a wife."

Lydia sighed heavily. "Will you listen to yourself? You speak of choosing a partner for life as if you were in the throes of choosing a horse. 'You' decided?" She practically spit the words at him.

"Well, of course, if you would rather I not . . ."

"I would rather we all be happy, Luke —

you, me and yes, Greta."

"I'm not sure she would appreciate your trying to replace Josef Bontrager in her affections almost before she's had time to get used to the idea that this might indeed be final and not one of his little tantrums."

To his surprise Lydia actually giggled. "He does have a tendency toward the childish behavior, doesn't he?"

Luke smiled. "You know as well as anyone that there is still every possibility that he will come to his senses and beg for her forgiveness."

"All the more reason for you to step in now."

"I do not follow your reasoning and besides . . ."

Yet another sigh of pure exasperation. "Luke, are you or are you not attracted to my sister?"

"We have already . . ."

"The truth," she demanded.

"*Yah.* Of course, but not in the way that you may think."

"Or is it not in the way that *you* won't allow yourself to think?"

Luke gritted his teeth. Lydia Goodloe with all her book learning was far too smart for him. She talked in riddles that made him uncomfortable. He fought hard to maintain his temper with her and then thought about years of enduring such probing conversations.

"I will say this only once more, Lydia Goodloe. If you do not wish to be out riding with me then say so and tonight will be the end of it."

For a long moment the only sounds were the night-calling birds, the clop of the horses' hooves on the hard-packed road and his own frustrated breathing. Then Lydia straightened on the wagon seat next to him and said softly, "I have taken care of Greta for most of her life, Luke. She is not only my sister — she is my responsibility. Our parents have died and we have no other siblings — other than Pleasant, our half sister. I only want what is best for Greta."

"And what is that?"

"Greta's attraction to Josef was never about her love for him but rather for the life he represented to her. A home that she could manage, children she could mother and raise — these are the things that my sister has dreamed of her entire life."

"I can see that, but where do I fit into this picture?"

Lydia looked directly at him for the first time since they'd boarded the wagon for the ride to town. "You could give her all of that, Luke Starns. And more importantly, you could give her a great deal more."

Luke met her gaze. "I'm listening."

"I believe that given some time you and Greta could love one another and even if not, you would provide her with the safe haven she needs — the kind of security to be herself that she has known with me all these years. Josef has never been able to accept her for who she is."

"And what about you?"

"I have a good life, Luke. I do not need more. Truly. But I worry about Greta and when she told me about what Josef had done, I realized that perhaps this time I could help her find another way. So I prayed last night and all through the day today for God to show me His will. And it seemed that every time I looked up from my prayers, you were there. I know that you protected her yesterday. I know how inquisitive Roger Hadwell can be. Before you know it, you are telling him things you hadn't planned to reveal. And yet I knew the minute I saw the Hadwells this morning that they had no idea anything had changed until the marriage announcements. They were as stunned as anyone else."

"Your sister suffered a terrible blow yesterday when Bontrager just quit her there in the middle of town, Lydia. It was not my business — much less Roger Hadwell's — to pry into that. I did only what anyone would have done given her state of distress when she entered my shop."

"And you have kept on doing such things. Tonight at the singing? Twice you intervened. Your instinct to protect her is apparent."

Luke sucked in a long breath and let it out slowly. "If you and I were to marry, Lydia, Greta would become my sister, as well. Of course, it would be my . . ."

"But if we married, Luke," she reminded him gently, "where would your heart be?"

From the day that he'd stepped off the train and settled in Celery Fields, the women in town had been planning a match for him and it was hardly a secret that their choice was Lydia. "You realize that in rejecting me you are going to disappoint all of Celery Fields?"

"They'll recover, especially if you will follow my advice and pursue my sister instead."

In that moment the front wheel of the wagon hit a deep rut and swayed. Lydia instinctively put out her hand to steady herself, clutching Luke's hand in the process. He spoke gently to the team of horses to reassure them but it was not the brush of Lydia's hand — quickly withdrawn — that he found himself recalling. It was the memory of Greta's fingers on his when they both reached for the tray.

Nonsense, he thought, shaking off the memory as he gathered his thoughts.

"Well," Lydia prompted. "What do you think?"

"I have stated this as plainly as I can, Lydia. If you prefer that I not call on you, just say so and we'll have no more of it. I do not need your assistance in seeking a wife."

"No, you don't. But Greta needs precisely such assistance in her quest to find a husband."

They had finally reached the Goodloe house and Luke called for the horses to halt. Lydia was down from the seat before he could make his way around the team to offer help. She stood on the first step that led up to the front door.

"Come and sit," she invited. "We need to work out a plan as soon as possible if you would be interested in a match with Greta," she said. Clearly in Lydia's mind they had both agreed to this incredible plan of hers to secure a groom for her sister.

"Lydia, I barely know your sister." But he

followed her onto the porch and took his place next to her in the weathered wooden swing.

"You know me no better, Luke, and yet you evidently felt you knew me well enough to escort me home this evening. Greta would be a good match for you. Far better than I could ever be. You and I are both of a more serious nature. I thank God every day for the blessing of having Greta in my life. She brings a certain joy to the lives of others that would certainly be missing if it weren't for her. It seems to me that you would be a man in need of her . . . lightness."

He smiled in the darkness. "Now who is the one speaking as if she were selling a horse?" he teased.

"There is a way that we could manage this so that no one would be the wiser. All of Celery Fields would assume you were courting me, and in the meantime you and Greta . . ."

Luke stood. "It's clear you want what's best for your sister, Lydia, but give her time to find her own way — her own heart."

"Very well. I will not pursue this any further this evening but I will ask that you think over what I have proposed. Should you decide against the idea, then I would accept that. Either way I want to thank you for the kindness and caring you have shown Greta. It is evident to me that you are a good man, Luke. A man that my sister — and I — can trust to do the right thing. Good night."

Luke waited until Lydia had entered the dark house. After a moment she lit a lamp. And he saw her in silhouette as she took a seat near the window and opened a book. Behind him one of the horses shuddered, setting the harness to jingling in the still heat of the night. Without climbing back onto the wagon, Luke led the team down the lane to his shop, and all the while he found himself thinking about the impossible idea that Lydia had suggested. Him with the vibrant and fickle Greta?

If ever he'd needed proof that God had a sense of humor, surely this was it. But he admired Lydia for her intense loyalty and love for her sister. And the truth was that he could not stop thinking about Lydia's plan — and how it might just work.

CHAPTER SIX

"What do you mean you rejected Luke Starns?" Greta demanded the following day when the sisters sat down for their evening meal after Lydia had come home from the schoolhouse. "You might at least give the man a chance."

"We are not right for each other, Greta. We are too much the same. There would be no . . . no . . ."

Greta had rarely seen her sister at a loss for words. "No what?"

Lydia shrugged and turned her attention to her soup. "No surprise, I suppose."

"You do not like surprises," Greta reminded her. "When I tried to surprise you on your birthday last year you were very cross with me as I recall."

"Greta, shocking someone out of their wits by springing at them from the dark with a cake lit by candles is hardly the same thing as getting to know another person and revealing hidden traits that are not at first evident."

"Don't use your teacher's tone with me," Greta snapped as she stalled for the time that she needed to translate what Lydia had just said. "Besides, isn't getting to know Luke exactly what is required here?" She felt triumphant to have found the chink in her sister's argument.

Lydia sighed. "You must trust my judgment in this, Greta. I know what makes my life content, what gives me pleasure and joy." She continued eating her soup as if they were discussing the weather.

"I don't understand you sometimes, Lydia," Greta groused. "And I have to say that I feel a little sorry for Luke Starns. It is obvious that he has taken some time to work up the nerve to approach you at all and then you reject him after one buggy ride?"

"We rode in a wagon," Lydia corrected, ever the stickler for the details.

"Wagon . . . buggy. You're missing my point."

Lydia looked at Greta directly. "What is your point, sister?"

"I . . . You . . ." Greta drew in a long breath, forcing her jumbled thoughts into some semblance of order and out came the one thing she had not expected. "Are the

118

two of us then to spend the rest of our days here — a couple of spinster sisters?"

To her surprise Lydia laughed. "Oh, Greta, Josef Bontrager is not the only candidate to court you. He has become a habit — one you should be more than happy to quit."

"I was not the one to quit this 'habit' as you may recall."

"No, he was. And I appreciate that you are hurt by his action — his cruelty. But the fact of the matter is that there is a man living right here in Celery Fields that I have come to believe would be the perfect match for you — and you for him."

Greta searched her brain for some logical candidate and found that no one came to mind. "Who?"

"The blacksmith."

"Oh, for goodness' sake, Lydia. I thought we were having a serious discussion about your future here. It is unlike you to make jokes . . ."

"I am quite serious, Greta." Lydia laid down her soupspoon and gave Greta her full attention. "Knowing that everyone had assumed Luke Starns and I would begin seeing one another, I took some time to study the man these last several months — to learn what I could of him through observation and conversation with others."

"And you decided he was not right for you. That does not mean that you can simply pass him off as if he were a book you'd started and decided you didn't care to finish."

"I am not passing him off, Greta. I had resigned myself to you and Josef marrying although I will admit to praying for God to ease my concerns for your ongoing happiness once the union took place. But now . . . Oh, sister, do you not see God's hand in all of this?"

It was rare for Lydia to become so impassioned — only when she believed that God was leading them did she exhibit such zeal and enthusiasm. But Luke Starns? And Greta?

"I have prayed long and hard on this and yesterday it seemed to me that God was guiding us in a direction that could not be denied. Just say that you will consider the idea, Greta," Lydia pleaded.

Greta hesitated. She could hardly admit that ever since she'd gotten past the announcement of coming nuptials and everyone's gasp of surprise not to hear her name called, her thoughts had turned more than once to Luke Starns. She'd told herself that her only interest in the man was in whether or not he could make Lydia happy. But during the night when her thoughts had turned to memories of his smile and the touch of his hand brushing hers, she'd feared that perhaps she was more attracted to Luke than she had allowed herself to admit.

She studied her sister's features for any sign that she was simply giving up before she'd given her own romance a chance to begin. Lydia met her gaze clear-eyed and with the expression of one who knows her own mind. "But what of Luke's feelings in the matter?" Greta asked. "Does he have no say in this?"

"I have spoken to him and he . . ."

"You what? Lydia, how could you?" The words were a shout in Greta's mind but they came out as a whisper of pure disbelief. "Have you completely taken leave of your usual good sense?"

Lydia pressed her lips together and frowned. "Since the day our dear *Maemm* left this world, Greta, I have been trying to do what I believe is in your best interest, what will give you a life that fulfills the potential that God endowed you with — a spirit filled with joy and happiness that you so brilliantly share with others. You are meant to be a wife and mother — that is so clearly God's plan for you. Luke Starns will make a good husband and father. He will be a mitigating influence on your more capricious disposition and you in return will bring out the lighter side of his nature. The man carries a burden of sadness, Greta. That much is plain to see. And you said yourself that he is pleasant to look at and . . ."

"What did he say?" Greta had left the table, her supper untouched. She paced back and forth before the windows that looked out over the town and Luke's blacksmith and livery business. "When you spoke of this with him — what was his response?"

"He agreed to . . . consider the idea." Lydia's voice was not nearly so self-assured as it had been earlier. "Greta, I see now that I may have overstepped, but . . ."

Greta whirled around to face her sister. "*May* have? Do you have any idea of what you have done, Lydia?"

Lydia stood, picked up her soup bowl and turned toward the sink. "As I have said, I have tried to do what I thought best for you, Greta."

"I am not a child," Greta said. "And I am not one of your students, Lydia. The man I thought I would marry has not been gone but a little over two days and you have already . . ."

Lydia set down her dishes then faced Greta squarely. "Tell me that you love Josef Bontrager," she challenged. "Tell me that you ever truly felt for that man what a wife should feel for her husband."

The one thing that Greta had never been able to do — at least not convincingly — was tell a lie. She bowed her head for a moment, trying to frame her response. "In time we would have . . ."

"You have been together for much of your life, Greta. If you cannot summon such feelings now, what difference was a ceremony going to make for either of you?"

Greta felt the need to defend Josef, especially because Lydia's words had a disturbing element of truth to them. "He is a good man. He has been a good friend . . ."

"He is all of that and more — a good provider, a man of faith. Do you love him? Have you ever truly loved him?"

It took Greta several moments to answer but only because she was reluctant to admit what she had known for some time now. Lydia waited patiently.

"No, but . . ."

Lydia rested her hands on Greta's shoulders. "And that is my point. You deserve to love and be loved, Greta. You have so much to bring to a marriage and home of your

123

own. Perhaps I have gone too far in speaking with the blacksmith. I see now that it was too soon — that you needed some time. And he may not be the right person at all. But I have prayed for your happiness for so long and last night when you were so upset at the singing I saw something quite unexpected."

"What was that?"

"I saw, sister, that Luke was upset for you."

"Of course. He looks upon me as a future member of his family — or at least he did. He thought that once you and he married we would be as brother and sister." She glanced out the kitchen window at the smoke rising from the chimney of Luke's business. He was still working although it was late in the day and all other shops were already closed. "I have to go and set things right," she announced.

She took down her bonnet from the hook by the front door and jammed it over her prayer *kapp,* not caring whether the pinned-up hair held. "I know you were only trying to help, Lydia, and I am grateful for that, but the idea that Luke Starns would have the slightest interest in me when everyone knows he had set his sights on you is ridiculous. You are understandably nervous about this entire matter of Luke courting you. But to turn the tables and try to convince him . . ."

"Please don't act in haste. Will you not pray on the matter first, Greta?"

"I will pray as I walk down to town," she called out as she left the house. "I will pray that God will give me the words to set this right again," she added in an undertone as she made her way down the sandy lane to where she could hear the rush of wind as the blacksmith pumped the giant bellows to stoke the fire.

Luke had thought of little else once Lydia Goodloe had laid out her idea that her sister Greta was the woman he should set his sights on. It was almost comical the way things had reversed. Back in Ontario the crafty father had sought a match for his elder daughter. Now the elder sister sought a match for her younger sibling. And in both cases Luke was in the middle of things. What plan did God have for him in all of this?

He pumped the large bellows next to his fire, noting how the exhale of air matched his own huffs of exertion and frustration. All he wanted was to settle down and start a family. That had always been God's plan for men like him — the responsibility to continue the line of the faithful, to do good works and to be a reliable member of the community. Why did that have to be so complicated?

"Luke Starns!"

He startled and nearly dropped the half-formed bridle bit that he'd begun to bend over the anvil. He glanced over his shoulder to find Greta Goodloe standing quite close to him, not more than a foot from the fire itself. She was tapping her foot impatiently and her arms were folded tightly across her body. From her expression he gathered she had been there for some time already.

"Careful of the fire," he said as he turned his attention back to his work.

She rolled her eyes. "I am not a child," she announced. "Although it appears that you and my sister have decided that I am. I am a grown woman and I will decide who I will permit to court me and who I will not."

Slowly Luke laid down the jig that he'd been about to use to break off an errant piece of metal. He glanced at her and fought a smile. The fact was that she looked exactly like a petulant child trying hard to appear grown-up. She was scowling up at him, her blue eyes glittering in the combination of the reflected light of the fire and late afternoon sunlight spilling in through the small window.

"I see you and your sister have discussed the matter," he said, turning again to his work mostly to hide his smile.

"My sister has taken it upon herself to manage my life for many years now."

"How blessed you are to have someone so concerned for your well-being."

She seemed to consider this and loosened the grip she had taken on her body with her folded arms. "Yes, well, she means no harm. Lydia is a good woman," she mused and then seemed to recall where she was and why she had come, "and that is all the more reason that you should see her suggestion that you and I . . . That we . . . She is testing you, Luke Starns."

He filed a burr from the bit. "How so?"

Her lips worked but no sound came out. She looked down at her black shoes and for the first time failed to meet his eyes directly. "It would be prideful of me to say so and that is not at all my intention but the fact remains that for all our lives people have thought of Lydia as the smart one and me as . . ."

Her voice trailed off.

"The pretty one?" Luke guessed.

She nodded once and then met his gaze.

"But Lydia does not see her own beauty. She is not only smart. She is kind and caring and when she smiles . . ."

"She is all of that and more," Luke agreed.

Greta let out a sigh of relief. "Then you see it, as well. Oh, Luke Starns, do not let her put you off. My sister deserves happiness."

"And what about you?" He had not meant to speak his thought aloud and yet there it was. Greta's eyes widened in surprise. "Forgive me, Greta," he hastened to add. "I should not have . . . We were discussing your sister."

"And you," she reminded him. "So, what do you intend to do about this turn of events, Luke?"

"Do? Your sister made her feelings plain last evening. She does not wish to spend her time with me."

Greta sighed heavily. "She does not know what she wants. The question is are you serious about finding a wife for yourself or not?"

"I am quite serious."

"Then . . ."

"What I will not do," Luke interrupted her, "is go after a woman who has declared openly that she has no interest in making a home with me."

Greta frowned, then took several breaths

as if preparing to say something. But the silence between them stretched on for a long moment. At one point she turned away and he thought she had decided to leave, but then she paced a few steps and returned. This time she found the words. "And what of her idea that you and I should . . ." She let the sentence trail off.

Luke set down his file and examined the bit. "That depends," he said slowly.

"On what?" Greta had placed both hands on her hips, a stance so defiant that Luke was tempted once again to laugh.

"On whether or not you are able to put aside your feelings for Josef Bontrager. Your sister believes that your feelings for him were not as strong as they should be for two people planning a life together. Do you agree?"

"Lydia is . . . I mean . . . Oh, I don't know," Greta replied. "How can either of you expect me to know what it is that I'm feeling these days? It's too soon."

"Then let me put this a different way. If Josef came to you and asked for your forgiveness and pleaded with you to reconsider, would you?"

She blinked up at him — once, then again, then a third time. And all the while she chewed on her lower lip. He could practically hear her thinking this through. "No," she finally whispered. "I would not."

In his chest Luke felt his heart pounding and he realized that over the months he had been in Celery Fields, he had taken more notice of the beautiful Greta Goodloe than he had allowed himself to admit. He had learned a hard lesson back in Ontario and he had been determined not to make the same mistake twice.

But if she had come to realize that Josef was not for her . . .

On the other hand, surely the idea that she might be firm in her decision to be rid of Josef did not mean that she was ready for someone new. He cleared his throat. "Then that is an important first step that you have taken toward coming to an understanding of exactly what God's plan may be for you."

"And what comes next?" she moaned.

"In your shoes I think that I would ask God's guidance for moving forward from here."

She seemed to consider this and then accept it with a nod. "And what of you and Lydia?"

Luke sighed. She was like a dog with a fresh bone, worrying the thing to death trying to get at the marrow. "I have taken your sister at her word, Greta. And having done so, I also must pray for guidance."

Greta smiled and with that smile it seemed as if her entire being relaxed. She glanced around the shop, her gaze once again reminding him of that image he'd had during services of the butterfly flitting from one thing to the next until she finally settled her attention on him. To his surprise she plopped herself down on the wooden chair as if settling in for a long visit.

"We're quite a pair, aren't we, Luke Starns?"

"How so?"

"Each of us being so certain that we were on the right path. Neither one of us prepared in the least for the bumps and gullies along the way."

This time when he smiled, he did not try to hide it from her. At the same moment he realized that in the short while since he had first become aware of her presence, he had felt the urge to smile several times. "You will find what you want — what God wants for you," he assured her as he went back to his work.

"And you?" She was nothing if not persistent. Luke could only imagine how her pursuit of a matter to its end must have grated on the fence-straddling Josef Bontrager.

He shrugged and concentrated on completing the bridle bit, more to avoid her eyes than because the work was urgent. She got up and wandered closer to the fire.

"Why do you not have more light in here?" she asked.

The abrupt change in topic was unnerving — as was his awareness of her nearness as she studied the work he was doing. "I need the shadows to distinguish the temperature and pliancy of the metal," he replied.

"How so?"

He took a length of scrap metal and placed it in the fire pit. "See the red? And now orange?"

She nodded.

"It will glow yellow and when it is white, then it will melt. I need to take it from the fire when it is somewhere between the orange and the yellow. We call that 'forging heat' — the point at which the metal can be shaped. Too much light can make it hard to see the change in color."

She was standing so near to him that if either of them moved an inch their sleeves would brush. In the glow of the embers, her face took on a radiance that made his heart beat faster. He took a step away. "You should probably be getting back," he said.

She walked toward the double doors but paused when she reached them. "You know," she said wistfully as she looked out toward the street that was deserted as evening began to settle over the town, "Josef was not simply the man I thought I would marry. From the time we were seven he was like the brother I never had. Oh, we had a half brother — Pleasant's brother. He was Caleb's *Dat,* but he died when I was very little and I never really knew him. So I relied on Josef. Josef and Lydia have always been my two best friends. Now there is just Lydia."

Her voice trailed off as she continued staring out at the street. He watched her for a moment, trying to decide if she might be shedding more tears over Bontrager. But she seemed calm and if not serene, then at least resigned. He wiped his hands on a rag as he walked to where she stood.

"I would be your friend, Greta Goodloe," he said softly.

She turned to him, the fading sunlight on her face. Her expression was one of bewilderment. Then without another word she walked out of the shop and back down the lane to the house she shared with her sister.

"I would be your friend, Greta," Luke repeated in a high falsetto voice that mimicked his own. "No wonder you are not yet wed," he groused as he returned to work.

All the way back to the house, Greta thought not about her own troubles or even about Josef. She found herself thinking about Luke Starns — the gentleness of his words, his offer of friendship. Lydia was right. He was a good man.

"Well?" her sister asked the minute Greta stepped into the kitchen. It was as if Lydia had been holding her breath the entire time Greta was gone.

Greta shrugged. "We talked a bit." She took down a jar of candied orange rind the sisters had put up the previous winter and selected one of the sweets, then held out the jar to Lydia who waved it away impatiently.

"And?" she demanded.

Greta shrugged. "He said that he will not pursue you if that's your wish." She sucked the sugar off the orange rind. "Of course, in my opinion, you are making a huge mistake."

Lydia snorted with derision. "This is hardly a matter for levity, Greta."

"I'm not laughing."

Lydia frowned. "I thought you went there to set matters straight regarding a courtship

134

with you."

"We discussed that, as well — briefly." Greta popped the last of the orange sweet into her mouth and then licked her fingers.

"Well, to what end did you discuss matters?" Lydia asked.

"I told him that I thought you had simply suffered a bout of nerves."

"I have suffered no such thing. I know my mind, sister."

"He seems to have accepted that. It would appear that the two of you are well matched in your determination not to be swayed."

This time the sigh that Lydia released was one of relief. "Well, at least there is that." She focused her attention on Greta. "But my concern is for you — you and your dream of starting a home and family of your own, Greta."

"With Josef."

"So you thought."

"So everyone thought," Greta corrected.

"Even so, it appears that God has given you — and Josef — a new direction. However that does not mean that His intent for your future has changed. Luke would make a fine husband and father. He is a good provider and a solid member of the community. You could not do better."

"Nor could you."

Greta almost laughed when she saw Lydia's mouth working but no sound coming out. Her sister was always at a loss for words on those rare occasions when Greta made a strong logical point. The role of teacher turned student was not a comfortable one for Lydia.

"But I will accept your decision in the matter," she added.

"Gut," Lydia announced, taking charge once more. "Then my decision is that you and Luke Starns will begin seeing one another for the purpose of determining whether or not this is the direction God is leading the two of you." She stopped Greta's protest with a raised hand. "In fact, while you were out, I came up with the perfect plan to give you both the time and privacy you will need to become better acquainted. Should things not work out, no one will be the wiser."

Greta sat on the edge of a kitchen chair, her chin in her hands. There was no sense arguing with Lydia. She would have her say and once she had spoken, Greta would do as she always had. She would go her own way. "I'm listening."

"As of last evening, the whole community thinks that Luke has begun his courtship with me," Lydia began. "That means that should they see you and Luke talking or walking together or riding somewhere together, they will not so much as raise an eyebrow. As my sister — and presumably someone who is helping the romance along — it is perfectly acceptable for you to be seen with Luke."

Greta was completely confused. "So, you are saying that you wish for Luke to court you after all?"

"No," Lydia exclaimed. "Don't you see? Because everyone will assume that he is courting me, you and he will be able to spend time together without any pressure or expectations." She drummed her fingers on the kitchen table as apparently a new wrinkle in her plan came to mind. "Of course, it will be expected that he will come to call on me in the evenings after you have retired for the night, but no matter. It will be dark and the two of you on the porch will look no different to anyone passing by than if I was the one sitting there with Luke. Yes, this will work beautifully."

"Aren't you forgetting one small thing, Lydia?"

"I don't think so. I have gone over this idea thoroughly and . . ."

"You do not have Luke's agreement — or mine — to pursue this." But even as she said those words, her mind had already begun racing with the possibilities that Lydia's plan could work for her. It would take the attention off her troubles and place the focus on Lydia and Luke. Besides, the limited time that Greta had spent with the man had not been unpleasant. Not at all. And she could possibly coach him in ways to pursue Lydia — ways that would make Lydia fall in love with him.

"Greta, I am asking you to give the idea a try. Where is the harm in that?"

Greta knew her sister well enough to understand that Lydia had made up her mind on this matter and would not be moved. "All right," she said. "If Luke Starns agrees to your plan then I'll do it."

But later that night long after Lydia had gone to sleep, Greta lay awake trying to work through the jumble of thoughts that came with the idea of putting Lydia's plan into action. Finally she threw back the light quilt and went to stand at her open window, hoping to catch a breath of air in the still steamy night.

And that's when she saw the smoke and then a flash of orange — a flame reflected in the window of Luke's shop.

"Fire!" she shrieked as she grabbed her shawl and ran toward the blacksmith's shop.

CHAPTER SEVEN

"Fire!" Greta shouted again and pointed to the blacksmith's shop when a sleepy-eyed Lydia stumbled onto the porch, barefoot and confused.

"I'll go to the school and ring the bell," Lydia told her, instantly awake and taking charge as she pulled on her shoes and grabbed her shawl. "You go and make sure that Luke is out and rouse the Hadwells and Yoders and others."

Greta took off, her loosened hair flying out behind her, her bare feet oblivious to the stones and calcified seashells that pocked the sandy lane. The smell of smoke was strong now and from inside the shop she could hear a horse whinny and the crackle of the flames. "Luke," she screamed as she started up the outer stairs that led to his living quarters above the shop.

Before she could reach the door, Luke emerged, hooking his suspenders over his shoulders as he ran down the stairs toward her. "Get back to your house," he ordered. "Go!"

In the background they both heard the clanging of the schoolhouse bell.

"There's a horse," Greta told him.

"I know. There are four of them. I'll take care of that. Just get away from the building now." He wrapped his arm around her and half carried, half propelled her the rest of the way down the stairs.

A buzz of voices coming their way told Greta that the school bell had done its job and those people living in town were up and responding. Roger Hadwell was already handing out buckets from his hardware store. Someone else was pumping water into a horse trough outside the burning building. A bucket line quickly formed — men, women, children all working in unison to fight the flames that now had broken through to the roof.

Seeing that there was nothing she could do to help the others, Greta ran back to the rear of the shop where she'd seen Luke head after he'd told her to go home — as if she could. As if anyone living in Celery Fields would stay in the safety of their own homes when a fellow citizen was in trouble.

He was pulling a terrified horse from the

stables, tugging on the rope as the horse dug in its heels and tossed its head, trying to loosen the rag that Luke had tied over its eyes to lessen the animal's panic. Luke had also covered the lower half of his face with a towel and now Greta did the same, pulling the end of her shawl over her mouth and nose as she ran toward the stables. Luke had said there were four horses. He had saved one, but the others must still be inside.

She ignored Luke's muffled shouts as she entered the stables where the fire raged at the front of the building. The rear stable area was filled with acrid smoke that stung her eyes and made her breathing come in labored huffs. She felt her way along the series of stalls, unleashing the remaining three horses and sending them one by one running free from the burning building, certain that Luke would be out there to calm them.

As she stumbled back into the yard of the livery, gasping for air, she saw Luke racing after the terrified horses as they dashed away in all different directions. "No!" he shouted as he chased one and then another to no avail. Then seeing Greta, he turned on her as he pulled down the wet cloth he'd used to cover his face. "What were you thinking?" he demanded as he took hold of her upper arms and stopped just short of shaking her.

"I was thinking we needed to get those animals to safety," she shouted above the din of the gathering crowd and the roar of the fire. Too late now she realized that in letting the animals run free she might have cost Luke a great deal more than the loss of his building and home. The horses were not his. He was providing livery service for their rightful owner. No wonder he was so angry with her. "I didn't think there was time . . ."

"You could have been overcome," he said, his face very close to hers. "You could have been killed."

It hit her then that what she had taken for anger was not that at all. His first thought had been for her — her safety, her well-being.

"But the horses — you would have lost . . ." She started to shake uncontrollably as it struck her that he was right. She had put her life at risk to save those animals.

He pulled her close, uncaring of who might take notice as he cradled her head in one large hand against his chest. "Sh-h-h," he said softly. "It's all over now. You're safe."

And as she gave herself over to his embrace of consolation she realized that in all the times that Josef Bontrager had held her, she had never once felt the safety and certainty that she felt now in the arms of Luke Starns. After a moment he stepped away but kept his one hand tangled in the thickness of her loose hair. Slowly he released her and then he took hold of the edges of her shawl and covered her hair and shoulders.

"Better?" he asked.

Greta managed a nod.

Behind her she heard a cry of alarm from the crowd fighting the flames and turned just in time to see one wall of the large structure collapse, sending a shower of sparks into the sky that was just beginning to show the first signs of dawn. She heard a horse's snort and saw that all three of the animals she'd set free had wandered back into the yard where they stood in a row, drinking from the trough in back of the hardware store.

Luke released a shuddering sigh and Greta took hold of his hand as they stood side by side, watching the uncontrollable fire. "You can rebuild," she assured him. "Everyone will help."

He stared at what had been his business and his home and nodded. "You should join the others," he told her as he gently pulled his hand free of hers and she knew that he was thinking of her reputation. Lydia was right. Luke Starns was definitely a man who thought of others before himself.

"You'll need a place to stay," she said.

"Something will turn up and it won't be for long." He smiled at her. "After all, this is Florida. I can sleep under the stars if need be and we can spend every day rebuilding."

She knew he would have no need to sleep outside and that in just a matter of days work would begin on rebuilding for that was the Amish way. Neighbor took care of neighbor. Luke's home and the source of his livelihood might lay in ashes today but it would not be long before he was back in business. The people of Celery Fields would see to that.

"Come on," she said, taking his arm and guiding him toward the main street where the members of the bucket brigade had faced reality and were standing together, waiting for the fire to burn itself out. As Luke approached the gathering, several men patted his shoulder while the women murmured their sympathies. Greta stood aside and let him be drawn into the circle of the townspeople.

"Is he all right?" Lydia asked, coming alongside her.

"He will be," Greta replied and in her heart she realized that she intended to make sure that this was the truth.

In the light of the new day, Luke stood at what had once been the entrance to his business and considered the smoldering remains. Dawn had brought with it a sky that was overcast and one that held the threat of rain. It occurred to him that God would send the showers to smother any embers that might lay hidden beneath the rubble. After that he could start the process of clearing away the rubble left after the fire. Roger had already stopped by to write up the order for the lumber and other supplies that Luke would need.

But as he stared at a thin thread of gray smoke rising from what had once been the stairway that led to his living quarters, he couldn't help but wonder if God had meant him to receive a different message from the fire. It was from the small kitchen at the top of the missing stairway that he had begun his study of Lydia Goodloe. From there he had watched her leave for the schoolhouse on the mornings when school was in session. He had watched her handle whatever chores needed attention outside the house while Greta apparently took charge of the cooking, laundry and cleaning chores. He had watched both sisters sitting on the porch after services or on the Sundays when there were no services reading or waiting — in Greta's case — for Josef Bontrager to come calling.

From time to time he would see Greta. Although he rarely studied her as he did Lydia. In those days he hadn't paid much attention to Greta. But he realized now that he had always been far more aware of the younger Goodloe sister than he had allowed himself to admit. She'd come out to the porch, say something to her sister and then take off walking toward town. Sometimes she would mount the bicycle the sisters owned and head off in the opposite direction toward the main road, toward Sarasota. Once or twice he had seen her return hours later and she would add a large whelk or conch shell to the border around Lydia's vegetable garden.

Today all that had changed. Today he couldn't seem to focus on anything other than the sheer panic he'd felt when Greta had run into the stables and not reappeared for some time. The way her hair had felt as it tumbled over his hand. The way her small thin body had felt cradled against his. The lightness of her and at the same time a strength that could not be named — or denied. When he'd looked around and seen her running into the stables — into the very heart of the fire — he had acted purely on instinct, running after her. But he'd not gotten three steps before he was stopped by first one horse and then another and another charging him as they ran for safety. And then there she was and seeing her he found that he could breathe again.

When he'd held her and she'd looked up at him, her eyes sparkling with tears brought on by the smoke and perhaps her own realization of the chance she had taken, the urge to kiss her had been almost overwhelming. So much so that he had stepped away. But he had not released his hold on her hair — thick and yet fine as silk, golden with highlights of red like the flames shooting up to the sky behind her.

Lydia was right. He had set his sights on the wrong sister. But how best to convince Greta of that?

"Luke?"

He stiffened at the sound of Greta's voice behind him. He might be clear now about his feelings for her, but she was still too close to Bontrager's betrayal. For that matter she might be in love with Josef. He forced a half smile and looked around.

"Thank you again for saving the horses," he said. "And to your sister for raising the alarm."

"It's still a total loss," Greta replied as she considered the pile of charred debris before them. "Have you found a place to stay until you can rebuild?"

"Haven't really thought about it. Something will turn up."

Greta released an exasperated sigh. "That's what you said last night. You're welcome to sleep in the loft of our barn if you like. Lydia said to offer."

Luke's grin widened. "She did, did she?"

"Don't get your hopes up," Greta advised, clearly mistaking his words for a sign that Lydia was softening toward him.

"I wasn't. I was just curious how you might feel about the arrangement."

"People will talk," she said with a shrug. "Lydia doesn't care one bit about what other people think or say but . . ."

"You do?"

She looked down. "Through no fault of our own, my sister and I have been the topic of gossip these last few days. I would like not to be in that position longer than is necessary."

He wondered if she was thinking about him holding her the night before. He wondered if perhaps someone had seen them and let Greta know that she had been seen in the arms of the man supposedly interested in her sister. "I'm sorry," he murmured. "The last thing I would want is to cause you — or your sister — distress. Tell Lydia that I am grateful for her kind offer but I will make other arrangements."

"*Denki,* Luke." She turned her attention more fully to the ruins before them. Carefully she walked closer, stepping over blackened wood as she reached down to retrieve one of his chisels. "Still warm," she said when she handed it to him.

"But still useable," he replied.

She smiled up at him and for a moment he could not find his breath. The business of being unable to breathe normally whenever Greta Goodloe was around was becoming an alarming habit.

"There must be more," she said. "Let me help you find them."

"Take care," he said as he followed her through the rubble. "There are still some live embers."

"I'll use this to move them," she said, holding up a piece of metal the length of a cane or walking stick. "Found another," she crowed triumphantly, holding up something that caught the sunlight. "We should have a contest to see which of us can find the most."

"We'll find everything when we haul away the debris," he reminded her. "There's no need to . . ."

"But that would not be nearly so much fun, Luke Starns. Do you not ever consider having a little fun?"

Fun? It sounded like a word from another language to Luke. He had been forced to maintain his focus on weightier matters for so long that solemnity had become a habit. How long had it been since he'd done something just for the pure pleasure of doing it? He moved a charred board with the toe of his boot and quickly uncovered three more small hand tools.

"Three to one," he called out as he set the tools in a pile.

"Unfair," Greta said but she was laughing and the sound was like musical notes. "You know what to look for — the shape and size and all."

"It was your idea," he reminded her as he held up two nails that he'd forged last week. "There are at least a dozen of these if that helps."

"Found one," she shouted and then quickly dropped the nail and shook her hand. "Hot," she admitted.

"Work in this area," he advised, motioning to the ruins where he stood. "Everything here seems to have cooled off." He had to force himself not to go to her and examine the possible burn to her fingers.

"Here's another — and another," she said as she took his advice and immediately found two more of the nails. "You'd best start searching, Luke, or I am surely going to be the winner."

Luke made a half hearted attempt to search the ground around his feet, but the truth was that the only thing he could look at was Greta's face hidden by her black bonnet and then turned up to him with that luminous, heart-stopping smile whenever she unearthed a new treasure.

He was considering the possibility that just maybe he might be able to persuade Greta to give her sister's plan a chance when he heard a shout from across the street and looked up to see Hilda Yoder bearing down on both of them.

"Uh-oh," Greta muttered. "We're in for it now, Luke Starns."

Greta straightened to her full height and folded her hands primly in front of her as she waited for Hilda Yoder to make her way from the dry goods store across the street to where Greta and Luke had been searching for things to be salvaged.

"Such levity after such tragedy," Hilda muttered, clicking her tongue in disapproval as she approached them. "Surely, Luke, you find no humor in the loss of your business."

"But I have not lost my business, Hilda," Luke explained. "I have only lost the building that housed it. I will rebuild and be back in business by month's end."

"Still, it hardly seems proper for the street to ring with laughter at a time like this." She frowned at Greta. "Do you not have things to do, Greta Goodloe?"

"Things to do?" Greta decided to play the innocent. She blinked her eyes at Hilda and was aware that Luke was fighting a smile.

"Shopping, ironing — whatever it is you do on a Tuesday morning."

"I had thought that such mundane chores might be postponed in light of our neighbor's loss," Greta replied. "I came to see how Lydia and I might best help Luke recover his losses. Lydia extended an invitation for him to lodge in our barn loft."

Hilda sucked in a breath that said far more than the stream of words she clearly was trying to swallow. But the very idea that two single women might house a single man, albeit in their barn, was clearly news that had shaken Hilda to her very core.

"It is a kind offer," Luke said, "and one that I have refused. I will seek other shelter."

"I should hope so," Hilda muttered.

"Perhaps you and your husband have a spare room?"

Greta had to bite her lip to keep from laughing out loud at the expression that passed over Hilda's face. So Luke Starns had a sense of humor after all. "The storage room at the back of the store," Greta suggested. "It would be perfect — close to everything he needs."

"I suppose that could be arranged," Hilda hedged. "But there's to be no cooking on the premises. We've had one fire and there's no need to tempt fate by setting the stage for another."

"There, Luke, you see. It's all settled. Hilda and her family will take care of housing for you while Roger Hadwell takes charge of organizing the supplies and labor necessary for you to rebuild as soon as possible. And the women will see to organizing meals to feed the work crews." She clapped her hands together and beamed at them both.

Hilda pursed her lips and glared at Greta. "Then may I suggest that you get on with your piece of this, Greta? The work crews will likely be here first thing tomorrow to begin clearing away this rubble and they will need plenty of water and sustenance if they are to withstand the heat."

"Right you are," Greta said as she turned to head to her house. "I'll get started right away."

"I'll send Esther to help," Hilda called after her.

Greta's step faltered only slightly as the full weight of Josef's betrayal hit her once again. "Yes, please do," she called over her shoulder, but she knew that her voice was too high-pitched to sound sincere. And she knew that, in her way, Hilda had as usual had the last word.

"Oh, why does she have to be so mean-spirited?" Greta fumed later as she and Lydia sat together, each doing a bit of mending before bedtime.

"We may be Amish, but we are none of us angels," Lydia reminded her. "You must include Hilda in your prayers for surely her unpleasant behavior comes from some deep-seated unhappiness."

Greta sighed. "You are too forgiving sometimes, Lydia. How about the idea that maybe she's just plain mean?"

"There is no such thing as being too forgiving and now I would suggest that you add a prayer asking God to forgive your sharp tongue when it comes to Hilda Yoder."

Lydia was right, of course. Greta's feelings toward Hilda — and Esther — were every bit as intolerant as Hilda's comments to her. "I will pray," she agreed, and then she smothered a giggle. "I do wish you could have seen the look on her face when Luke suggested that he could stay with her."

Lydia concentrated on her needlework, but she was smiling. "It would appear that in the aftermath of Luke's tragedy, you have come to a different opinion of him?"

Greta was surprised to feel herself blushing. "He is more . . . complicated than I first thought."

"Truly? In what way?"

"He has a lighter side. One we have not been aware of before now. Before he always seemed so solemn and stiff, but today . . ." Her voice trailed off as she recalled the lighthearted way that she and Luke had challenged each other to find the salvageable pieces of his business. "And how odd that it should be revealed once he has suffered such calamity."

"Perhaps it was not the fire and his losses there that stirred this lighter side of his disposition," Lydia mused. "Perhaps there was another cause — one that was quite unexpected."

"Must you always speak in riddles, Lydia?"

"All right, in plainer language, I am saying that perhaps his interactions with you — of which there have been several in just the last few days — are responsible for his lighter disposition."

Greta was struggling to find the words to tell Lydia how ridiculous that theory was when there was a knock at the door. It was past dark — past the time when someone might come calling unless there were some emergency.

Lydia set aside her mending and carried a lamp with her to the door. As she opened the door and lifted the lamp, Greta was surprised to see Luke standing on their front porch.

"*Guten abend,* Luke Starns," Lydia said and Greta was sure she did not imagine the hint of humor that brought a lilt to her sister's voice.

"I have come to discuss your idea," he announced without bothering with the usual polite greetings. "Could we — you, your sister and I . . ."

"If you are referencing the suggestion that you and my sister could take advantage of this time when all of Celery Fields believes that it is me you are calling upon to become better acquainted . . ."

"Yah," Luke said, cutting Lydia off mid-sentence.

Lydia turned to Greta. "You know, sister, I find that I am suddenly quite weary." She set the lamp back on the table. "Be so kind as to offer our guest a glass of that wonderful lemonade you made this afternoon. *Guten nacht,* Luke . . . Greta."

And before Greta could say anything, Lydia had entered her room and closed the door with a firm click, leaving Luke standing on the porch and Greta to deal with him.

"A glass of that lemonade would be welcomed," he said softly, "that is if you would ask me to stay."

Without a word she headed for the kitchen as much to gather her wits for this meeting with Luke Starns as to prepare the beverage for him. What could Lydia have been thinking? What was Luke thinking showing up unannounced like this? Had the world gone completely mad? It would seem so. Well, there was nothing to be done but for her to set things right again.

CHAPTER EIGHT

While Greta went to get the lemonade, Luke remained standing at the door. He was having serious second thoughts. It had taken him most of the evening to work up the nerve to come here. He should have taken more time to consider his purpose — develop some plan. He had no idea at all what he would say to Greta once she came out to the porch with the lemonade. He had thought it would be the three of them — that there would be the buffer of Lydia's presence to make the entire discussion take on the trappings of a business meeting. Now he was to be alone with Greta.

Greta — who was certainly taking her time getting lemonade for him. He peered into the darkened hall that led to the kitchen, but could see nothing so he sat down heavily in the wooden swing. He leaned forward, his forearms resting on his knees as he debated simply getting up and leaving. Coming here had been a mistake.

The screen door creaked and she backed her way out, holding the door open with her hip as she balanced a tray set with two tall glasses of lemonade and a plate of ginger cookies. Luke sprang to his feet to hold the door and then relieve her of the tray. "You needn't have gone to so much trouble," he said as he looked around for where he might set the tray. Other than the swing, the porch was bare.

"On the step," Greta said as she lifted the glasses and waited for him to set down the tray before handing him one. Their fingers brushed and for an instant her hand shook and the liquid sloshed dangerously close to the lip of the glass before she steadied it. "Please sit while you have your lemonade," she said with a nod toward the swing.

He did as she instructed, grateful to have anyone else making decisions about how this encounter might go now that he had come here with no thought other than to accept Lydia's offer to spend time with Greta. He left plenty of room for her to join him but she settled herself on the top step next to the tray and offered him the plate of cookies.

"Did you make these?" he asked, taking one. Now both hands were filled — one holding the glass and the other the cookie. Luke had never felt so awkward in all his life. He sat back, inadvertently setting the swing in motion and causing the lemonade to spill over his hand and the front of his shirt.

Greta was on her feet at once, using the tea towel that had lined the tray to dab his fingers and shirt, blotting the sticky liquid. Every attempt she made only made things worse as the swing rocked back and forth.

"Hold still," she ordered as she reached to relieve him of the glass and hand him the towel. But as he clumsily tried to assist her, the swing bolted like a skittish horse and she came tumbling onto his lap as the glass flew out of his hand and the rest of the lemonade showered them both.

At first, as he tried to help Greta off his lap, he thought that the gurgling sounds coming from her were a sign of how distressed and embarrassed she was. "I'm sorry for my clumsiness and for upsetting you, Greta Goodloe," he said. "I should not have come."

She raised her face to his then and in the soft amber light from the living room, he saw that she was not upset. She was laughing, her eyes sparkling with a glint of mischief. "Oh, Luke, don't be so serious. It

160

was an accident — one I had as much part in as you did. As the *Englischers* might say, it looks like we have broken the ice — or at least the glass." She nodded toward the broken pieces on the porch floor.

Luke felt the bubble of laughter rising in his throat and before he could stop it, he was chuckling with her as together they bent to pick up the pieces of the glass and set them on the tray. When the deed was done, Greta sat back on the swing next to him and handed him the tea towel. "I don't think it will stain badly — not if you add a little white vinegar when you wash it."

With one foot he pushed the swing into motion as he wiped his hands on the towel. "I'll remember that," he said.

"Who does your laundry anyway?" she asked.

"I do. My mother died when I was just a boy, leaving my brothers and my *Dat* and me. We learned to do for ourselves."

"My *Maemm* also died when I was little. We had Pleasant though and of course, Lydia was older by a few years, so she taught me."

"So, we have this in common. Do you remember your mother?"

"Not much. I was only three. Sometimes I think that it's only the stories I heard about her over the years that I call memories."

"*Yah.* I was older than you, but through the years . . ."

"Your *Dat* never remarried?"

"No. We kept busy with the farm and the business. Time passed."

"Your father was also a blacksmith?"

"*Yah.* He taught me his trade."

"And your brothers?"

"They took to the farming more. It suited them once they married and started families."

She was quiet then and her silence made him all that more aware of her closeness. She was so small and slim that if they had sat closer there might have been room for a third person on the swing. She smelled of soap and the zest of the lemons she must have sliced for the lemonade. He was beginning to relax and enjoy the quietness of the night, the nearness of Greta Goodloe, when she spoke again.

"You never married, though. Were you not tempted?"

And there it was — the one topic he had dreaded from the day he'd left Ontario. Should he tell her the entire story and accept the fact that once she heard it, she would want nothing more to do with him?

Or should he stick to the plan he'd made the day he'd left a letter of farewell for his father and brothers and left Ontario for good? The plan to start fresh and leave the past behind.

"I mean," she added when he said nothing right away, "there must have been . . . opportunities. Surely the single women in your community saw . . ."

He forced a smile and shrugged. "I never gave them a chance," he said with a chuckle. "Growing up without a mother — or sisters — I guess I learned to be on my own."

"Until now. Now your plan is to convince Lydia to marry you."

She stated this with such assurance that he was momentarily taken aback. Had she not understood why he'd come? Had Lydia not spoken with her about this? Of course she had. Greta had come to the wreckage of his business earlier that very day to discuss the matter.

"I no longer wish to marry your sister, Greta. I wish to marry you — if you'll have me." There. It was said. There could be no misunderstanding now. He found he could not look at her as he waited for some response. If she burst out laughing — as he'd noticed she had a tendency to do — he would simply stand up and walk back to the dry goods store where Hilda Yoder had set up a cot for him.

But she did not laugh. In fact she did nothing more than sit there beside him, still as a stone. Then she picked at some bit of string on her apron and he thought perhaps she had at last composed her reply. But she said nothing.

"If you do not wish," he began.

"Are you always so impatient, Luke Starns?" she snapped. "I am well aware that you and my sister think this the best possible plan for all our futures. What I don't understand is why. You had set your sights on Lydia and just like that, when she rejects you, you have turned them on me?"

"You were not . . . available for me to consider earlier." He chose his words carefully, but clearly not carefully enough for Greta.

She was on her feet in an instant, wheeling around to face him, hands planted on her slim hips. "I am not 'available' now, Luke Starns. I can understand my sister's role in this. She has taken charge of my well-being from the time we were both children, but you? What am I to you?"

Several answers to that question sprang instantly to mind — sunshine, loveliness, laughter and lightness among them. But he said none of those things. Instead his wounded pride overcame his true feelings and he stood, as well, towering over her as he brushed past her on his way to the porch steps.

"If you do not wish to even consider . . ."

"I did not say that," she replied, stopping him in his tracks.

"You confuse me, Greta Goodloe."

"Gut." There was the hint of a smile in her tone. "For you confuse me, as well."

He fought a smile of his own. Without turning to look back at her, he asked, "And is that a place where we might begin? Perhaps as friends?"

"I have already mistaken friendship for love, Luke. I will not make that mistake again. They are not the same thing." Her voice was so soft and filled with sadness.

"Do not equate me with Josef Bontrager," he warned.

"Josef believed we could build a future together. Now, apparently so do you. I really cannot see much difference. In both cases it would seem that you men decide when it suits you to take a wife — mostly for the purpose of starting a family and perhaps companionship . . ."

He was back onto the porch, his hands grasping her shoulders in an instant. "Stop it," he ordered. "Your sister is the one who has suggested a match between you and me. She has also plotted out a way for the two of us to become better acquainted without the barrier of gossip and speculation. I have given it considerable thought and it seems to me that this is worth pursuing. Celery Fields is a small community and if, in the end, we only come away with a friendship, doesn't that carry its own reward?"

He eased his hold on her and forced his breathing to steady. And then she did the very last thing he might have expected her to do. She stood on tiptoe and gently kissed his cheek. "You make a good case, Luke Starns. I will sleep on it and give you my answer tomorrow."

And then she was gone, the screen door closing behind her with a soft click and then the front door. Luke stood there for a long moment, his fingers touching the place where she had kissed him, his heart hammering so hard he doubted seriously that he could make it back to the dry goods store. Instead he sat down on the top step and absently picked up a cookie from the plate she'd left behind.

He chewed slowly, savoring the spicy crispness. Greta Goodloe had one thing in her favor for any man considering her as his wife — she made the best ginger cookie that Luke had ever tasted.

In her room Greta undressed and pulled on her ankle-length cotton nightgown. She straightened the gown's long sleeves and then carefully folded her clothes for use the following day. And all the while she was thinking about Luke. She crossed her arms over her chest and held onto her shoulders, remembering how his hands had felt when he'd gripped her there earlier.

For an instant she had thought he might kiss her. More to the point she had hoped that he might. She shook her head at that realization. What kind of woman was she that she could so easily leave all thought of Josef behind and turn to this stranger instead?

But Josef's touch had never aroused in her these feelings. Luke's simple act of placing his hands on her shoulders had provoked turmoil of her heart and mind.

Greta fell to her knees beside her single bed and clasped her fingers tightly together as she bowed her head and prayed for God's guidance. "I am so very confused," she admitted aloud. "About Josef and now Luke and . . . well, just everything. I want to follow the path You have set for me but I

167

honestly don't understand which turn to take." She unclasped her hands and pounded her fist on the soft mattress. "Help me," she whispered. "Show me the way." And then she thought better of her words. "Show me *Your* way," she amended and quickly added prayers for Lydia and Pleasant and her family and even Josef. "And Luke," she added finally. "He has suffered the loss of his home and business in one event. But more than that he seems to carry a heavy burden of loneliness and sadness. Whatever life he left behind when he came to Celery Fields troubles him still."

Her eyes sprang open as she realized that Luke Starns had not offered her his friendship out of pity. He had offered it out of his own need to find someone he could talk to and trust. What had he said? Something about friendship being its own reward?

"Oh, Greta Goodloe, you do suffer from the sin of self-importance. Surely God is showing you that it is time — past time — that you stopped thinking always first of your needs and dreams and place your attention on others." At first light she was determined to be up and putting into practice her newly established guide for life. She would serve others, always with an eye to making their lives better — and she would begin with Luke Starns.

"You seem to be in unusually good spirits this morning," Lydia said as she nodded her thanks for the breakfast that Greta had set before her.

Greta understood that this was her sister's way of inquiring about what had happened on the porch after she retired. "Did Luke stay long?" Lydia added.

"I am indeed in good spirits, and no, Luke did not stay long." Greta took her place across from Lydia. She reached across the table and took Lydia's hand as both sisters bowed their heads. After a moment Greta released Lydia's hand and picked up her fork. "After all," she continued as if there had been no interruption, "it is a beautiful day that we have been given. We must be sure to make the most of it."

She saw Lydia arch one eyebrow, her skepticism evident in that subtle gesture. "And how do you intend to do that?"

"I will go first to the bakery and work out an order with Pleasant for the breads, rolls and other baked goods we will need for the raising of Luke's stables and shop. Then I will visit the other women in town to see if I can recommend what to prepare for the men and boys working on the rebuilding."

"Everyone will simply bring what they can," Lydia said. "You know that."

"I do, but so many families have left Celery Fields that there will be fewer sources for the food and baked goods we'll need. I just want to see if I can persuade the women in town to focus on the basics. That way whatever those living in the outlying areas can bring what they like."

"You've given this quite a lot of thought," Lydia said.

"I have. It's taken my mind off . . . other things. Besides everyone is busy right now and as I mentioned we are shorthanded. Does it not make sense to be more organized under such conditions?"

"It does." Lydia studied her as if she were looking at a complete stranger. "Did Luke say when the rebuilding might begin?"

"No." Greta added a note to the list she had begun. "I should ask Roger Hadwell when the lumber and other supplies will be delivered. Of course, in the meantime there is the work of removing the remains from the fire." She glanced up at Lydia. "Could you let the children — the older ones — out of school early so they might help?"

Lydia set down her coffee cup. "I do not know what has stirred this spirit of goodwill in you, Greta, but I must say that it becomes you."

Greta could not hide her surprise at receiving such praise from Lydia. More often than not, Lydia was gently chiding her for her tendency to dwell too much on her own small problems when there were others suffering around her.

"It's high time I stopped feeling sorry for myself and concentrated on others," Greta announced and then she grinned. "Wouldn't you say so? Oh, that's right, you have said so many times."

Lydia smiled and set aside her napkin as she rose to gather the satchel that held her school supplies. "Let me know when you need the help of the older children and I will excuse them from class," she said as she headed for the door where she paused. "Well, it would seem that the work may go faster than we had thought, Greta. Luke and Roger are already unloading supplies."

Greta ran to the door. "Then there's no time to be wasted," she announced as she reached for her bonnet. "Come on, Lydia, I'll walk partway with you and go first to the bakery."

She was well aware that Luke had paused in the unloading of the beams and other lumber stock to watch as she and Lydia walked down the lane toward town. Halfway along, Lydia took the path to the school-house while Greta continued on her way to her half sister's bakery. As she passed Luke and Roger, both men nodded briefly in her direction and then turned their attention back to their work.

"Heard you saw Lydia Goodloe home from Sunday's singing," Greta heard Roger say as the men transferred the lumber from the wagon and stacked it in a pile near the foundation of Luke's shop.

She strained to catch Luke's reply but could only hear a mumbled response — a response that had Roger chuckling.

"Pleasant?" Greta called out as she entered the bakery.

"Back here."

Greta followed the smells of cinnamon and yeast to the large kitchen where Pleasant prepared the goods that she sold. On one long table were loaves of bread dough rising in their pans. "I am way ahead of you," Pleasant announced as she wiped her hands on her apron. "I thought we'd start with a dozen loaves and then add to it as necessary."

"Pies," Greta began and before she could say more Pleasant pointed to the large wood-burning stove.

"When I saw Roger Hadwell taking in that delivery this morning I knew we would be getting started tomorrow morning once everyone has finished the milking and other chores."

Greta consulted her list. "I thought I would ask the other women in town for side dishes and casseroles."

"I could speak with Hilda Yoder and Esther," Pleasant offered.

Greta sighed. So word had spread about Josef flirting with Esther at the singing. "No. I'll do that. How many men do you think will come to help?" She was determined to change the subject, determined to turn Pleasant's pitying look away.

Pleasant shrugged. "Jeremiah and I were just talking about that last evening. It's hard to believe how the community has shrunk these last months. And it's been a while since there's been any call for raising a new barn or house or shop at all."

"Maybe some of Luke's customers from Sarasota will come to help," Greta said. "He's built a good business with them."

"He has at that, but the *Englisch* have a way of thinking that once they've paid for a service there's no need to do more. I wouldn't count on that if I were Luke."

"I didn't say he was counting on it," Greta

said, knowing she sounded peevish.

"How are things going between Lydia and him?"

"She hasn't really said." It wasn't a lie. Indeed Lydia had told Greta nothing about her conversation and the ride home from the singing with Luke. "I expect he's going to have other things to think about for a while."

Pleasant laid a pie pastry over the dish, pressed it into place and crimped the edges, all the while her lips were working with no sound coming out. "What do you think about a match between those two?" she finally asked.

Greta could not have been more surprised at the question. In general Pleasant had always viewed Greta as far too flighty to try and hold a serious conversation with.

"I don't know," she replied, trying to gauge Pleasant's mood. "They are both . . ."

"Serious to the point of being almost solemn, even grim. I was in a marriage like that before Jeremiah came into my life. I would not wish that for Lydia."

"You disapprove of Luke Starns?"

"Not at all. He's . . . Well, the truth is that he's far too much like me and like Lydia. Where will they find the laughter and the lightness that is so very very important in a marriage?"

"Luke is nothing like Merle Obermeier," Greta said softly. Everyone in Celery Fields had been well aware, when Pleasant had married the widower, that the man's sole purpose had been to find a mother for his four children. He had not loved Pleasant; in fact there were rumors that he had been quite cruel to her before his sudden death left her alone to manage a farm that was deeply in debt and four small children who had now lost both their parents. That's when Pleasant had returned to the bakery and that's when Jeremiah Troyer had come into her life.

"No, he is nothing at all like Merle was, but you cannot deny that he has a certain somberness about him, bordering on sadness. Does Lydia even care for the man? I mean in a romantic way of speaking?"

"Surely it's too soon for either of them to know," Greta protested, suddenly afraid that Pleasant might make her feelings known to Lydia — and Luke — and disrupt Lydia's plan for Greta and Luke to become better acquainted. For an instant she considered revealing Lydia's idea to Pleasant but then thought better of it. The fewer people who knew about it, the easier things would be when it did not work out.

"You mark my words," Pleasant said, continuing to line pie pans with pastry, "those two will either make each other miserable or they will come to their senses and understand that going their separate ways makes more sense — for both of them."

"I'm sure Lydia will find her way," Greta said, always loyal to her elder sister.

"He's awfully good-looking," Pleasant mused and then she giggled.

"Why, Pleasant Troyer, wait until I let Jeremiah know that you said such a thing."

"You didn't let me finish. Luke is very good-looking in that dark, mysterious way he has, but he can't hold a candle to Jeremiah. Now there's one fine-looking man."

Greta considered the differences between Luke and her half brother-in-law and found that, in her book, there certainly was no contest. Luke Starns won every time. But she wasn't about to say so to Pleasant. "Have to go," she said as she headed out and crossed the street to the dry goods store. But not before she glanced over to the hardware store, saw that Luke was nowhere in sight and felt a twinge of disappointment rise in her chest.

CHAPTER NINE

Over the next several days, Luke spent every hour of daylight clearing away the remains of his destroyed building. Lydia sent the older boys from the school to help him in the afternoons and Greta provided cookies and lemonade. Finally the day came that the framework for the shop, livery and his living quarters would be raised. Luke was awake well before dawn wondering how many men would come to help. How many were left to come? And of those, how many were able-bodied and young enough to manage climbing the scaffolding and straddling the beams as the building took shape?

He stepped out the back entrance to the dry goods store where he'd spent the last couple nights sleeping on a cot. He splashed water over his face and neck. It was going to be a hot day. The haze that hung heavy over the town was a sign that by noon the temperature was likely to be well into the eighties and the humidity would be even higher. He was glad of the wide flat brim of his hat as he set it in place.

As had become his habit he glanced toward the Goodloe sisters' house. Now that his shop was gone, he had a clear vision of the place from the porch of the dry goods store. He wondered what Greta was doing. The evening before, he and several others in town had helped her and Lydia set up long rows of tables in the Goodloe barn. That's where the workers would take their meals. He'd been touched by Greta's assumption that there would be a host of men ready to go to work and in need of sustenance as the rebuilding progressed.

She had that way about her — a way that refused to believe that everything wouldn't work out for the best. In spite of her near hysteria when Josef Bontrager had broken off with her, Luke had begun to understand that her reaction was less about being heartbroken and more about being embarrassed. Bontrager was sure to show up today and Luke couldn't help but wonder how Greta would handle that. For that matter he had to consider how he would handle working alongside the man. Bontrager was known for his carpentry skills and he would be a valuable member of the crew. It was going to be important for Luke to set aside his personal feelings toward the man.

He'd taken to having his breakfast — a hard roll and a cup of coffee — at the bakery since the fire. He liked Pleasant Troyer, although her disposition was nothing like her given name. Pleasant was known for stating her mind and most of the time Luke found that refreshing. Unfortunately that was not the case on this particular morning. She seemed determined to ferret out information about his past.

"Quite a difference in weather I'd guess between September here and what you were used to back in Canada." She set the roll in front of him and slid a dish of orange marmalade across the table.

"We could already have some cold weather by this time of year, that's certain," Luke replied as he poured fresh cream into his coffee and stirred it slowly.

"You had a shop back there, as well?"

"It was my *Dat*'s business."

"But you left there to come here." The statement rang with the unasked question: *Why?*

Luke took the last bite of his roll and licked his fingers. He smiled at Pleasant. "Like you said, the weather. Got to go." He left coins on the table to pay for the roll and coffee and escaped, but not before he saw the scowl that wrinkled Pleasant's forehead.

He heard the creak of wagon wheels and the plod of horses and looked up to see several dozen men parking their vehicles along the main street. As they stepped down from their wagons or buggies, they reached for their tools — aprons that held a variety of nails, toolboxes loaded with hammers, saws, tape measures and T squares. They talked in low voices as they gathered in small groups, each group assembling around one man that they had selected as their leader. In one group that leader was Josef Bontrager and Luke was grateful that the man had come to help.

From the opposite end of the street came the sound of several motorized vehicles and Luke saw trucks loaded with men — some that he recognized as his *Englischer* customers from Sarasota — pull up next to the hardware store.

Luke was unexpectedly moved by the arrival of these non-Amish men because he was well aware that many of them had lost their jobs when businesses in Sarasota went under and others were trying to make ends meet by working two jobs at low wages. And yet they had set their own worries aside to come and help him.

Overall there were far too many men to count but Luke would guess there were at least fifty or sixty of them. With this many skilled laborers, they would have a good start on rebuilding his shop by sundown.

"You gonna stand there gawking all day, Starns, or put us to work?" one of the *Englischers* teased.

Within an hour the work was underway. By sundown the frame of the building would be in place. Greta and the other women had transformed the Goodloe barn into a feast of casseroles, cold cuts, salads, baked goods and cool lemonade. At noon several men took their plates and moved down the line cafeteria-style. Luke couldn't help but notice how the *Englischers* were suddenly shy with the women around. "Thank you, ma'am," they would murmur without looking up or smiling.

The men would eat in shifts so that the work could continue until dark forced them to stop. Luke saw Greta moving among this first shift, refilling their glasses from a large tin pitcher of water, its sides sweating as the ice melted in the noonday heat. He saw that she was coming to the group of Amish men where Josef was sitting and wondered what she would do. Her smile never wavered as she bantered with the men and refilled Josef's glass. Luke felt such respect for her at that moment. Bontrager barely acknowledged her, maintaining a running conversation with another man until Greta had turned away.

But then Luke saw the way Josef's gaze followed her. Was the man having second thoughts? And if so, what would Greta do about that?

"Back to work," somebody called out and as one the men rose, set aside their plates and glasses and returned to the building. Luke turned to set down his plate and found Greta standing not two feet away, her face wreathed in a smile.

"It's going so well," she exclaimed. "Look how many men came from Sarasota to help — and on a workday for them."

"I have Jeremiah to thank for that," Luke admitted, having learned that Pleasant's husband had let it be known among the men he worked with at the local ice plant that their help would be welcomed.

"And your customers came, as well," she reminded him. "You'll be back in business in no time at all, Luke."

The way she said it Luke felt certain that she was right. That was the thing about Greta. She always seemed to see the positive in life. The way she was smiling up at him now made him feel like he could do just about anything he set his mind to doing.

"Luke Starns, we cannot work if we do not know what you want," Josef Bontrager said. He had returned to the barn and was standing there, hands on hips as he glared at Luke.

"Coming," Luke said and handed Greta his plate and glass. His good spirits plummeted when he realized that her smile had faded and her eyes were on Josef, not him. "Fool," he muttered to himself as he strode away from the Goodloe barn into the hot and steamy afternoon.

The men took another break in the late afternoon. By that time Greta and the other women had cleared away all the leftover food and washed and dried the dishes. Most of the women left shortly after the lunch had been served. There were chores to be done and children in need of their naps. As the sun moved lower in the western sky, Greta and Pleasant's stepdaughter, Bettina, moved among the workers, offering them cookies and cold milk. Greta was all too aware that Josef's gaze followed her wherever she went. If she spent too much time lingering over conversation with any one of the men — even the married ones — that gaze became a glare. More disturbing than that was the fact that Luke Starns also seemed to be watching her — and he appeared to be no more pleased than Josef was with her behavior.

Well, let them gawk all they wanted. Greta was so very tired of trying to live up to somebody else's ideal of how she should conduct herself. She liked people. She found the sheer variety and diversity of them a source of endless fascination. Wasn't it amazing how God had given each of his creatures their very own unique qualities? If Josef — and Luke, for that matter — chose to view her behavior as inappropriate, that was hardly her problem. Josef had made his choice and as for Luke — well, if he wanted to be her friend, or more than that — then he would just have to accept her for the way she was. After all, that's what true friends did.

"Greta?" Josef had come alongside her and was handing her his water glass. "Would it be all right if I called on you this evening?"

The very last thing that Greta had expected was this. Calling on her after dark meant — well, it meant that he wanted to pick up again with courting her. Didn't it?

She eyed him carefully. "Why?"

Josef chuckled nervously. "Do I truly need a reason?"

"Truly you do," Greta replied.

"Do not make me plead with you." In an instant Josef's tone had gone from a chuckle to an order.

"I am not making you do anything, Josef. Lydia has . . ." She fumbled for some excuse.

Josef frowned. "Of course. I had heard that the blacksmith was calling on her," he said. "Perhaps tomorrow?" He walked away without waiting for her to answer. She realized that he simply assumed that sooner or later she would agree to see him.

Using Luke and Lydia as her excuse had not been at all what Greta was about to say but since Josef's assumption had ended this awkward conversation Greta was thankful. Thankful that was until she saw Luke staring at her from across the yard and then turned to find Esther Yoder glaring at her, as well. So many people looking at her — all of them seemingly unhappy. Well, Josef had approached her. For once in her life she could not be accused of flirting. She picked up the last of the dishes and headed for the barn.

■ ■ ■ ■

As Luke watched Greta and Josef it occurred to him that he might just be walking right into the situation that had gotten his heart broken back in Ontario. It occurred to him that Greta Goodloe might have agreed to Lydia's idea to make Josef jealous. If that was her plan then it appeared to be working. Josef Bontrager had been unable to take his eyes off Greta all through the lunch break in spite of Esther Yoder and her mother hovering around him, making sure that he had second helpings and a large piece of shoofly pie. By late afternoon the man had clearly found his courage to approach Greta.

Luke was not given to jumping to conclusions. He reminded himself that he had no knowledge of the conversation that had passed between Greta and Josef. As he set in place the large heavy-notched beams that formed the support for the roof for his business, he went over every detail of what he had observed. Josef's approach. Greta's polite smile — or had that smile been one of expectation? Did she still have feelings for the man? How could she not? It had been less than a week since their break.

He was a fool on a fool's mission. Perhaps God did not intend for him to marry at all. Certainly the signs pointed toward that. The business in Ontario. Lydia's outright refusal to even consider a courtship. Had he become so desperate to marry that he had fallen into the trap once again of being someone's pawn in a game he did not wish to play? Was Greta's intention to use him to win back Josef?

"Well, we'll just see about that," he grumbled to himself as he dropped the last beam into place and signaled to Roger Hadwell at the other end of the log that it was secure. He scrambled down the scaffolding and stood with the rest of the crew to consider the day's work. The frame was in place for the building and the roof. Where that morning there had been nothing but barren ground, there now rose a skeleton of fresh-hewn wood and the men standing around him had done it all.

"I'd say that's a good day's work, Luke," one of his customers from Sarasota announced. "By the end of next week at this rate I expect you'll be in business." The man clapped Luke on the back as he and his friends headed for their trucks and drove away.

Luke glanced toward the Goodloe house

and saw Lydia coming home from her day at school. He wanted to thank her for letting the older boys come help with the work but he knew approaching her now would cause tongues to wag. Everyone assumed that they were courting — that much was evident by the sly comments some of the other men had made in his presence throughout the day. He saw Lydia pause for a moment and gaze at the structure. She called out something to the cluster of men nearest to her and kept on walking. Greta was nowhere in sight.

"Shall we offer a prayer of thanksgiving?" Bishop Troyer asked and all of the men gathered around the church leader as he offered up a prayer thanking God for the blessings of the day.

As soon as the prayer circle ended, those men that had remained for the whole day headed for home — some in their wagons or buggies and others walking, all promising to return the following day after chores to continue the work. Luke stood in the middle of town and watched them go and for the first time since coming to Celery Fields he felt like one of them. He was no longer a stranger in this community. His decision to rebuild his business, when it would have been just as understandable —

given the dwindling population and customer base — for him to leave Celery Fields and start over somewhere else, had secured him a place among the others as one of their own.

"Luke?"

He was surprised to see the bishop's wife coming his way. Mildred Troyer was a spry woman of indeterminate age and always ready with a kind word and a smile. She was much beloved by everyone in town and she had made Luke feel welcome from the day he'd first arrived. Now she handed him a package wrapped in brown paper and tied with string.

"I thought you might have use for these," she said. "I had to guess at the size but used our nephew Jeremiah's measurements. It seems to me that you and he are about the same size. If they won't do, you just bring them right back to me and we can alter them."

Luke loosened the string and pulled back one edge of the paper to reveal a stack of clothing — two shirts and a pair of trousers. Every bit of clothing he owned other than what he'd been wearing had been lost in the fire. He'd been making do with washing out his one shirt every night before he went to sleep and carefully brushing the day's dirt from his pants.

"Can't have you calling on Lydia Goodloe in clothing you've spent the day working under this hot sun in," Mildred teased with a twinkle in her bright blue eyes.

"Thank you. I never expected . . ."

Mildred patted his hand. "It's just neighbors helping neighbors," she assured him and then she went to join her husband for the short walk home.

Luke watched them go — two people who had spent more of their life together than they had with anyone else. They walked side by side, exchanging bits of conversation. They would share their supper and then sit for a while. The bishop would probably read or work on his next sermon while Mildred did some mending or quilting. Then they would go to bed — to the bed they had shared for so many years and through good and bad times.

Luke wanted that life. He wanted that one person he could trust to be there through everything. He wanted to know that at the end of his workday he would go home to that kind of comfort and companionship. He turned his attention back to the Goodloe house. A thin stream of smoke rose from the kitchen chimney. Greta was preparing supper for herself and Lydia. She must be almost as exhausted as he was for she'd been up early organizing the meals for the workers, making sure everyone was fed, clearing away and washing the used dishes.

He closed his eyes and pictured her in that kitchen, her laughter like music as she went about her cooking. He thought about her hands — hands he had held in his when he had removed that splinter — hands that knew how to work but that were still smooth and as soft as a baby's cheek. And from there it was an easy leap to thinking about children — his children — their children.

He shook himself free of his revelry and headed back to the dry goods store with his bundle of clothing. The women in town were taking turns feeding him, leaving a tin bucket with a cold supper for him in the evenings. They would do that anonymously for it was not the way of the Amish to seek recognition or praise for their good deeds. Sure enough, waiting on the back stoop of the dry goods store was a picnic hamper so filled with food that the top would not close all the way.

He sat on the step and opened it, suddenly ravenous. Inside were three pieces of fried chicken wrapped in waxed paper, a bowl of cabbage slaw, another of three-bean salad, and on top of it all a generous serving of chocolate cake. Sitting next to the basket was a thermos filled with sweet iced tea. Luke leaned against one of the posts that supported the covered stoop and began pulling the chicken apart with his fingers. Whoever his benefactor was tonight, she was the best cook in all of Celery Fields — at least as far as he'd been able to judge.

He thought about the women that had come that morning with their husbands, carrying their baskets of food up to the Goodloe barn to be set out for the workers. He mentally ran through the dishes the women had served as the men moved down the line filling their plates. There had been the chicken and the side dishes and of course, the bread, but that chocolate cake had not been served at noon. For dessert there had been a variety of pies, but no cake. As he savored every bite he thought that he would give a lot to know who had baked that cake for him.

And then he remembered. At the lunch served after services the previous week, when he'd tasted Lydia's terrible peach pie, Lydia had said something about Greta's chocolate cake. "If you like that pie," she'd commented as he savored the piece of pie she replaced her own with, "just wait until you taste Greta's triple chocolate cake."

"Triple chocolate?" Luke had asked.

"Chocolate cake, chocolate cream filling and chocolate butter frosting," Lydia had explained, ticking off each item on her fingers. "My sister has a weakness for chocolate."

Luke studied the remains of his piece of the cake. Was it possible that with everything else she'd had to do today, Greta Goodloe had also prepared supper for him? And if this was indeed her chocolate cake, then why had she not served it at the lunch? Was there some message in the fact that she had reserved a piece for him?

"One way to find out," he said as he packed up the remains of his picnic and drank the last of the tea. Normally he would simply leave the container and dishes from his supper on the stoop and the following day it would be replaced by that day's meal. He could only assume that the women somehow had figured out how to return the previous day's dishes to their rightful owner. Tonight though, he intended to be the one to return the used dishes — and if he was right about their owner, then just maybe she would offer him a second piece of that cake.

Greta had told herself that she was simply

overtired. That's why she had gone out to the porch to sit awhile after Lydia had retired for the night. It certainly wasn't because she expected Luke to come calling. The man had barely said ten words to her all day. And between the fire and the days spent preparing to rebuild, courting was surely the last thing on Luke's mind. And besides, who knew what the rules for courting were where he came from? Amish communities could differ greatly in the manner in which the people conducted themselves. Maybe in Canada . . .

The house was dark but there was a moon and light enough for her to see the stark silhouette of Luke's new building. *Courting.* Were they actually going forward with Lydia's plan? Had Luke agreed? Had she?

"*Guten abend,* Greta Goodloe."

She had been unaware of him coming up the path, so lost had she been in thoughts of the day just past and her confusion about what she wanted in all of this.

"May I sit with you?"

"*Yah,*" she said, her voice barely a whisper as she made room for him on the weathered porch swing.

He set down the basket that had held his dinner. "I would hope there's some of that chocolate cake left," he said and in spite of the darkness she heard the lilt of lightheart-edness in his tone.

His teasing gave her confidence. "What makes you think we have chocolate cake to offer?"

He chuckled as he settled next to her, fill-ing the space so completely that there was less than an inch between his shoulder and hers. "Your sister once told me that you made the best chocolate cake in all of Celery Fields. I just assumed that the piece I had tonight for my supper was from your hand. I could not imagine a more delicious cake, but if I have guessed wrong then perhaps one day . . ."

She jabbed him with her elbow. "Stop teasing me. The cake was mine although there are any number of women in Celery Fields that might have given you its equal."

"Somehow I doubt that." Luke pushed the swing into motion and the two of them sat in silence for a long moment, all hint of lightheartedness replaced by their shared realization that they were here side by side in the dark.

"Tell me about the seashells," he said finally. "I saw you return with one for the garden the other day. Where do you find them?"

"In the bay."

"The bay?"

She studied him, trying to see if he was still teasing her. "The bay between the mainland and the barrier islands — the keys that separate the mainland from the Gulf of Mexico."

"You go there? Alone?"

"Sometimes. I like going there. It's very quiet and peaceful. There are wonderful birds and of course, the shells — some of them are still occupied and it makes me laugh to see them scuttling around in the shallows."

"I would like to see that."

An idea came to her. "We could go — the two of us. Everyone thinks that you are calling on Lydia so if you and I went down to the shore together, no one would be surprised. It's perfectly normal for you to be seen with me as Lydia's sister. Do you want to go there one day?" Suddenly her mind was filled with the image of Luke walking with her through the shallow waters of the bay, examining the sea life, watching the birds. It was an image that filled her with joy. "Perhaps this Sunday afternoon?"

Luke's hesitation gave her pause. As usual she had rushed in with a plan not fully considered. How did she know he was even interested in courting her at all? Perhaps he

196

still had his thoughts set on Liddy. "Forgive me, Luke. Sometimes I . . ."

"I would like to walk at the shore with you, Greta. I would like that very much."

The warmth that swelled in Greta's chest spread to her lips as they parted in a smile of delight. "You could fish there, as well. Many of the men and boys from Celery Fields fish there."

Luke laughed. "I'm afraid I'm not much of a fisherman, Greta."

"Then we will simply wade in the water and study the sea life and perhaps be fortunate enough to find an unoccupied seashell to add to Liddy's collection."

"How is it Lydia's collection when it would seem that you are the collector?"

"It's something I do to help her. She likes taking the different shells to the school to show her students and they make a lovely border for our kitchen garden. Liddy can name every single shell. She is so very smart about such things."

"But does she make the community's best chocolate cake?" Luke asked.

Now it was Greta's turn to laugh. "You are still determined to have a second piece, are you?"

"I am — and a third tomorrow if there is any left."

Greta stood up. "Very well. Wait here and I will cut you a slice, but after that . . ."

He caught her hand as she turned toward the door. "And will you sit with me while I eat the cake, Greta?" He ran his thumb over hers.

"I will," she agreed and as she gently pulled free of his touch and entered the house, her heart sang with what she could only define as giddiness. She liked Luke Starns — she liked him a great deal.

Luke found himself smiling broadly as he leaned against the porch swing, his arms spread across the back of it. He listened to the sounds of Greta in the kitchen — taking out a dish and cutlery, uncovering the cake, pouring a glass of milk or water to wash down the cake — and he found that he liked those sounds very much. More than that he liked the image of Greta Goodloe in the kitchen preparing something just for him.

He closed his eyes and thought about how his life had changed in only a matter of days — the fire and then the way the community had come together to help him rebuild. The business with Lydia and now calling on Greta. He thought about how sitting so close with her on the swing he had been more aware than ever of the sheer life force that seemed to radiate from her petite frame and touch everything around her with its energy and power. In all of his life Luke had never felt so alive as he did in the presence of Greta Goodloe.

He closed his eyes and prayed silently that he truly understood God's plan for his life and, if that plan included the possibility of a life spent with Greta, then God had surely blessed him. He heard her come onto the porch, the screen door closing with a soft thud behind her. He made room for her next to him on the swing and held out his hand to take the plate she offered.

In the light from the window he saw that she was smiling and he thought that he had never in his life seen a woman so very beautiful as Greta Goodloe was. *"Das ist gut,"* he managed around a large bite of the cake.

"So happy not to disappoint you," Greta replied as she set a glass of milk on the floor near him and sat down next to him. She sighed heavily. "Do you truly wish to do this?" she asked.

Aware that they were no longer discussing the merits of her chocolate cake, he set the plate next to the glass of milk and gave her his full attention. "Do you? I saw you talking to Josef earlier today and . . ."

"It is unlikely that I will be able to avoid talking to Josef now and again," she snapped irritably.

"I did not mean it as an accusation."

She pushed herself more firmly back onto the swing and folded her arms. "He asked to call on me."

Luke was confused. "I thought that he and Esther Yoder — that . . ."

"Josef is a man who has difficulty choosing what he truly wants."

Luke took a moment to consider this. "But surely, in the matter of choosing a wife . . ."

"He's always afraid that there might be something better — someone better."

"Then he is a fool."

"And are you any different, Luke Starns? You set your sights on Lydia and yet here we sit. What about that is so very different than Josef deciding to consider Esther?"

Any comparison between him and Josef Bontrager was insulting in Luke's mind and his lips hardened into a straight line as he stood up. "Thank you for the cake — for the supper tonight, Greta. I can see that your sister and I have not given you the time you need to consider whether or not your feelings for Josef . . ."

"Please do not try and hide your wounded

pride under the veil of pretending that this has anything to do with my feelings for Josef. I will admit that I am still reeling from the events of the last several days, but I know my mind, Luke Starns."

Luke bristled. "This is not a matter of wounded pride," he protested.

"Then what?"

"I like you," he blurted. "Your sister saw before I did that I noticed you long before Josef quit you. In time I think that perhaps we could . . . that I could come to . . ." He ran his hand through his thick hair as he struggled to find the words. "The fact is, Greta, that . . ."

She was standing next to him now and in the lamplight he saw that she was smiling. "The fact is, Luke Starns, that you are seriously seeking a wife. My sister has spurned you and you have turned to me — also spurned. We make quite a pair."

Under the light of her smile and her softened tone, he felt all of the tension drain from him. "We do at that," he admitted.

And suddenly they were both laughing — laughing so hard at the ridiculous situation in which they found themselves that they were unaware of a buggy passing the house on its way out of town.

CHAPTER TEN

Over the next two weeks, Greta and the other women once again set out the lunch for the men as they finished construction of the outer walls, laid the floor for the hay loft and framed out new living quarters for Luke. As soon as the last shingle was in place on the roof, the men would go back to their farms and businesses and jobs in town and Luke would work alone with the occasional help of neighbors as they had time. There would be no further need to organize meals for the crews of neighbors and customers from Sarasota. Once the last dish had been washed after the last shift of men taking their noonday meal before returning to work, the other women gathered their belongings and headed for home, leaving Greta alone to finish cleaning up.

She stretched her back as she stood at the kitchen door of the house that her father had built before she was born and watched the men working. By sunset the roof would be complete. Within another week Luke would be back in business. She saw Luke walking across the high roof as easily as if he were walking on firm ground. He carried a stack of shingles and she heard the sound of his laughter as he set them down and began to work next to Roger Hadwell.

She also saw Josef glance to where Luke was working. He'd been about to start up one of the ladders leading to the roof, but then he had turned toward Luke and back to where Greta watched from her porch and stepped away from the ladder. He'd set down his hammer, wiped his hands on a cloth before drinking a dipper of water and starting across the yard toward her.

Greta steeled herself for the confrontation that was bound to come. It was clear to her that Josef had changed his mind about pursuing Esther Yoder. Pleasant had confided that news to her earlier when Greta had wondered what might be keeping Esther and Hilda from coming to help serve the workers.

"He quit her just last evening," Pleasant told her. "She is devastated, of course, and Hilda is furious."

Greta sighed as she watched Josef approach. So, he had changed his mind after all. Well, he was too late. The realization struck her like a bolt of lightning as she realized that her mind was made up. The idea that she needed to make a choice between Josef and Luke was no longer a matter of concern. Of course there was no way of knowing whether or not things would work out with Luke in the end. But for now she was more certain than she had been of anything in a very long time that it was God's plan for her to give a courtship with Luke the time necessary to see where it would lead.

"Did you need some more lemonade, Josef?" she asked when he reached the foot of the porch steps.

"I need to know why Luke Starns was sitting — laughing — with you and not your sister on your porch the other evening."

Greta's heart beat a staccato rhythm as she tried to come up with some plausible answer that would not jeopardize Liddy's plan to give Greta and Luke the time they needed to get better acquainted. "You must have . . ."

"It was not your sister's laughter I heard — only yours, Greta — and his. Lydia was nowhere in sight."

"She was inside," Greta replied. It was not a lie. "Were you spying on my sister and me, Josef Bontrager?"

"I was driving by on my way home — a fact you might have taken note of were you not so engaged with the blacksmith. I have to wonder what Lydia thinks of your spending time with him?"

"She thinks that it is fine," Greta said. "Not that it is any of your business. This is a private matter, Josef."

"He is not courting Lydia. He is calling on you." The way Josef's eyes widened Greta understood that he had finally worked out the details to their logical conclusion.

"Again, this is none of your . . ."

"You will not deny it?"

"I will not discuss it."

"Because denying it would be a lie and you do not lie, Greta."

Before she could form a reply, Josef had turned on his heel and stalked off. She watched as he returned to the construction site, packed up his tools, offered some explanation to Bishop Troyer and then drove away.

Once again Greta felt her chest tighten with the certain knowledge that by morning everyone in Celery Fields would know that Luke was calling on her and not Lydia. Once again she would be the topic of speculation and gossip. Oh, why did life have to be so very complicated?

After Greta told him later that Josef had uncovered their secret, Luke decided to take a ride out to the Bontrager farm. His plan was unclear. He knew only that Greta had been more than a little upset and he wanted to protect Greta from becoming the topic of fresh gossip in the community. She'd been through enough and through no fault of her own. What was Bontrager's problem? Hadn't he been the one to quit Greta? Hadn't he been the one to make it no secret that he had turned his attention toward the Yoders' daughter?

The Bontrager farm was an impressive expanse of plowed fields laid out like a patchwork quilt around a large white farmhouse, a whitewashed barn and other outbuildings. The property lay along a rushing stream and was surrounded by a split-rail fence. When Luke saw what Greta would not have, his heart went out to her. He thought about how she would have thrived in this place, turning the house into a home, the large yard into a playground for the children, the kitchen garden into her own private store of herbs and vegetables.

Forcing himself to contain the rising irritation he felt with Josef Bontrager for being such a fool, he tied his horse to a hitching post and walked up the path that led to the front door.

"He's not there," a voice shouted.

Luke turned to see Josef's Uncle Cyrus standing in the doorway to the barn, a piece of straw dangling from the corner of his mouth.

Luke retraced his steps since it was obvious that the older man had no intention of moving toward him. "Any idea when he'll be back?"

Cyrus shrugged. "I expect it'll be some time — maybe a couple weeks. He left this morning. Asked me to watch over things 'til he returned. Something about needing to make a visit up north."

"I hope no one in the family has taken ill," Luke said and meant it.

"Nobody I know of and I do keep up with all of them wherever they are." Cyrus's tone was defensive. He squinted at Luke. "He owe you money or something?"

"No. I just . . . It can wait until he gets back." Suddenly a thought had come to Luke that made his heart race with excitement. With Josef gone — possibly for several days or even a couple weeks — he and Greta would have the time they needed to discover whether or not they were right for each other unencumbered by her concerns about Josef exposing them. Luke headed back across the yard to where his horse was tied up.

"Kind of sudden his leaving," Josef's uncle remarked and Luke realized that the man had followed him. "Seemed kind of upset about something."

"He probably just had a lot on his mind and wanted to be sure this place was looked after," Luke offered as he mounted his horse.

"Could be. More likely it's something to do with the Goodloe woman. He thinks he made a mistake there."

"Well, it was his decision," Luke said through gritted teeth.

"*Yah,* that's true. I expect that he was thinking that as a practical matter a union with the Yoder girl made more sense — financially speaking. After all, these are hard times for everybody and Josef has got himself a big nut to crack running this place. The Yoders — as everybody knows — have a real steady business. Secure."

Luke understood what the man was saying. Joining forces with the Yoders made more sense financially speaking than marrying Greta who had no dowry at all.

"But the heart knows," the older man

continued, "and that boy's heart has always been set on Greta Goodloe." He shook his head as he turned and ambled toward the barn. "I'll let Josef know you came around once he gets back."

Luke nodded and turned his horse toward town. He could not wait for evening when he could walk up to the Goodloe house and tell Greta what he'd learned. He wondered if she would see it as the opportunity that he did. Only time would tell — and thanks to Josef Bontrager's sudden decision to take a trip, they now had that time.

"I hope nothing's gone wrong with his family," Greta said that evening when Luke told her about Josef's trip. "Maybe somebody's sick."

"I asked, but I didn't get the idea that it was anything like that," Luke told her. "His uncle certainly would have known if somebody in the family had taken ill, don't you think?"

"I suppose. But then where could he have gone? I mean to just take off like that?"

"Maybe he needed some time to sort things out. Seems to be common knowledge that he's regretting his decision to quit you."

Greta considered this as she and Luke sat side by side on the porch swing, the lamp in the window casting a pale golden light over them.

"Are you regretting his decision, Greta?" Luke asked and she realized that his voice had softened to the point where it was barely above a whisper.

"It was his decision," she said firmly.

"But he might have changed his mind and that's not an answer."

Greta had to wonder if all men were like this — always questioning what her feelings might be, what they were going to be in the future. Josef had done that repeatedly, taking every conversation she had with any male and turning it in his mind into a flirtation or abandonment of him. "What are you asking me, Luke Starns?" she demanded irritably. To her further annoyance the man actually grinned. "What's so amusing?" She sounded like Lydia now — Lydia would say something like that.

"Which question do you want me to answer?"

"Both."

"All right. Second answer first — I was smiling because when you get your dander up you are a little like a spoiled child."

"I seem to have to repeatedly remind you that I am not a child," Greta snapped. "I am a grown woman — grown up enough to have been jilted once and now maybe yet again."

"I have no intention of jilting you, Greta."

She noticed that any hint of amusement had disappeared from his tone. "Then what?"

"When I learned that Josef had gone away for a while, it seemed to me that perhaps God was giving us this opportunity."

"What opportunity?"

"To become better acquainted without the shadow of Josef Bontrager hanging over us. To consider whether or not your sister is right in her estimation that we could make a good union and to do it all before Josef returns. That way if things between us do not work out, you know that Josef . . ."

"Don't you dare say that he would be willing to take me back as if I were some flawed piece of farm equipment or something."

Luke surprised her by taking her hand between his larger ones. "Listen to me, Greta, and hear me clearly. There is not a flaw in you that I can see. If things do not work out for us it will be because you found flaw with me — that you realized that a union with me would not make you happy."

She studied him, his features now fully revealed in the lamplight and realized that he was serious. "And how will we know this?"

He ducked his head for a moment and his thick, dark hair fell across his forehead. Greta had to resist the urge to brush it back with her fingers. When he looked up he was smiling and that smile had a way of making her heart beat a lot faster than was normal. "I suggest that we could start by thinking we might wed, then we could spend these evenings talking about what being married to each other might look like."

"What it might look like? I don't understand."

"You know, we could imagine how we would be together, what we would do, what we would talk about, what things we share in common and how we may differ."

"And then?"

He tossed his head like a horse clearing the errant strands of hair. "I don't know. I mean I just came up with the idea this afternoon after I learned that Josef had gone away. Don't you see? It's like God is giving us the time we need to figure this all out."

It gave her comfort to see in his expression and hear in his voice that he was as confused about this entire business as she was. But like Lydia he had laid out a plan — one that just might work — while she had come up with nothing at all.

"Very well," she said, pulling her hands free of his and sitting back in the swing so that they were side by side but no longer facing each other. "How do we begin?"

There was a moment of silence that stretched on for long enough that she glanced his way and saw that he was smiling — yet again. Then he stood up and held out both hands to her.

"What?" she demanded as she came to her feet and realized the two of them were fully concealed in darkness now.

"Well, I was thinking that in courting it's sometimes getting that first kiss out of the way that can break the ice, so to speak. You know, it sets both parties more at their ease not having to think about when or even if it will happen."

"You wish to kiss me?"

"Very, very much," Luke said huskily as he drew her closer. "If you would agree."

His mouth was no more than a whisper's distance from her own and she realized that she had raised onto her toes to meet him halfway. "I think that would be a good start," she said.

"Das ist gut," Luke murmured as his lips skimmed hers.

Greta and Josef had kissed, of course.

After all, they had been a couple for most of their teen years. But Josef's wet, almost desperate kisses were nothing at all like Luke's full lips touching her face. His kiss darted and teased as his lips met her lips and then skittered to her cheeks and onto her eyelids, squeezed shut to savor the experience. And just when she thought that her knees might buckle with the sheer pleasure of being in his arms, he tightened his embrace and kissed her fully on the mouth for what seemed an eternity and yet was over in an instant.

"Das ist sehr gut," he whispered as he pulled her to him, her hands trapped against the broadness of his chest. His mouth now rested close to her ear and his breath came in audible gasps as if he had just run a very long way to reach this place.

Beneath her hand she could feel the steady thumping of his heart. It reminded her of that day in his shop when she had watched him pounding out the bridle bit. She snaked her hand between them until she had freed it enough to comb her fingers through his hair.

"Again," she said and smiled when she heard the rumble of his laughter. She looked up at him. *"Bitte?"*

A shudder ran through his entire body as

he cupped her jaw in his palm and tilted her face to his. This time when he lowered his lips to hers, there were no teasing forays onto her cheeks and eyelids. Instead their mouths collided in a burst of warmth and need that Greta realized was exactly the kiss that she had imagined sharing with the man she would marry. A lifetime in Luke's arms? She did not even need to think twice about it.

When he pulled back a little, she actually whimpered in protest. "I think that we have done a good job of getting that first kiss — and the second — out of the way," he said, "and now we can go forward with truly getting to know each other and deciding if there's a future for us."

"If you kiss me once again," Greta teased as she stroked his cheek, "I think there may be no need for discussion."

His laughter rang out in the silence of the night as he set her back on the swing and collected his hat. "We will discuss," he said as he bent and kissed her cheek in a purely brotherly — and disappointing — way. "I want you to be very, very sure of whatever decision you make." He walked back toward his shop then and as he went Greta heard him humming softly to himself.

Greta sat on the swing alone for a long

time after Luke left. She repeatedly ran her tongue lightly over her lips, tasting the kisses she'd shared with him, remembering the way she had fit so perfectly in the curve of his arms. She relished the realization that while his kiss had nearly been her undoing, her kiss had caused that shudder of pleasure she felt rocket through his chest and shoulders.

But she reminded herself sternly that a few shared kisses were not a solid foundation for a lifetime spent together. Luke was right. They barely knew one another and if she didn't want to make the same mistake she had made with Josef — a man she had known perhaps too well — she was going to have to do something to remedy that.

"A frolic," she said aloud. "It's the perfect solution."

Frolics were events where the entire community came together to complete some project — sometimes frolics involved only the women when they gathered for a quilting bee, for example. But she had to come up with something that would involve the entire community — male and female.

Lydia agreed when Greta presented her with the idea the following morning. "The schoolhouse could use a fresh coat of whitewash and a good cleaning," she suggested. "I'll send word home with the children today. We can plan it for a week from Saturday."

Greta frowned. "But then how will Luke know?"

Lydia's eyes twinkled mischievously. "Well, we will have to order the whitewash from Roger Hadwell and it seems to me that he does enjoy spreading news of all sorts."

"He does at that," Greta agreed and giggled. "I'll go and order the whitewash this morning."

As it turned out there was no need to rely upon Roger to tell Luke about the frolic for when Greta walked into town she saw the two men sitting outside Luke's shop.

"*Guten morgen,* Greta," Roger called out as she came around the corner of the livery.

"And to you," she replied, but it was all she could do to keep her eyes on Roger when all she really wanted to do was look at Luke. Was it possible that she was so very fickle that she could so easily be drawn to this dark stranger when it had been just a week and a half since Josef quit her?

She focused her attention on Luke's hands, the fingers long and thick, and could think only of how those palms had felt cradling her cheeks the evening before. "I . . ." Her voice failed her. She felt a fire ignite in her cheeks as if he had touched her now. She cleared her throat. "Liddy is announcing a frolic to clean and whitewash the schoolhouse a week from Saturday," she said, spilling out the words in one breath lest she lose her voice once again.

Roger pushed himself to his feet. "Whitewash, you say? I think there might just be some leftover from when we last painted the house." He headed for his store. "Coming?" he asked when Greta did not make a move to follow him.

"Yah," she said and glanced at Luke for the first time since encountering the two men. "In a minute," she added, her eyes locked on his. She realized that he seemed to be as nervous as she was about this encounter in broad daylight. "Lydia was wondering, Luke Starns," she began in a voice that even she realized was too loud, "would you have the time to come and help? I don't know if you have frolics where you're from back in Canada, but . . ."

Roger had paused on his way back to the hardware store and was studying her curiously.

"We do have frolics," Luke said softly. "I'll be there."

Three simple words, accompanied by a smile that set her heart to racing, was a promise she could count on.

"Denki," she murmured softly, but inside she was singing as she followed Roger to the hardware store.

CHAPTER ELEVEN

News of the frolic to clean and paint the schoolhouse spread quickly. Lydia reported that she could hardly keep the children's mind on their lessons because they were so excited about the event. For the citizens of Celery Fields — as indeed for all people of the Amish faith — work was rarely if ever considered drudgery. Greta had sometimes marveled at the way *Englischers* complained about having to take on the simplest tasks. More than once she had been helping Pleasant in the bakery and served a visitor from Sarasota who sighed happily over the fact that "At least I don't have to bother baking bread or making dessert for my family. I don't know how you can do it day after day in this heat."

For Greta the woman's comment had come as a complete mystery. She could not wait for the day when she could bake and prepare meals and keep house for her husband and their brood of children. She had been preparing the meals and managing the house for her father and Lydia for years now and in the process she had earned a reputation throughout the town as an accomplished cook. Unlike the *Englischers,* who tended to spread compliments around like so much chicken feed, those of Amish faith did not believe in receiving or giving compliments. That would lead down the path of prideful ways. Thinking well of oneself or of something done well was a sin. But Greta could tell by the way the other women of Celery Fields were always glad to see her arriving at some function with her basket, or how the men belched with satisfaction after enjoying one of her cakes, that God had blessed her with the gifts to do everything associated with managing well a home and family.

On the Saturday of the frolic, she smiled as she waited for the chunks of bittersweet chocolate to melt on the wood stove and thought about the night that Luke had come asking for a second helping of her chocolate cake. Then she closed her eyes as she relived, for perhaps the hundredth time, the taste of his lips on hers. She thought about little else these days other than Luke Starns. When would she see him again? What was he thinking about as he went about his work or lay alone in his restored upstairs apartment at night? And most of all she wondered when he might kiss her again.

Her nose told her that the chocolate was burning and she opened her eyes with a start and grabbed for the pan with her apron-wrapped hand. There was nothing so sweet as the scent of chocolate warming on the stove and nothing so rank as the odor of that same chocolate burnt to a tarry mess. She dropped the pan in the sink and pumped water into it, making a face as the combination of cold water on the hot ingredients only intensified the acrid smell.

"That's what you get, Greta Goodloe," she chastised herself, "for daydreaming and not minding the task before you. Now it's ruined and you'll have to start again and there's no time to get the cake made and properly baked before . . ."

"Greta?"

Luke stood in the kitchen doorway, filling the space with his broad shoulders. "Who are you talking to?" He glanced around.

"Myself," she admitted. "I was baking a cake for the frolic and I got . . ." Her eyes focused on his mouth — a mouth that seemed to be fighting a smile — and she found that she was having trouble breathing much less finishing a thought or sentence.

He wrinkled his nose as the odor of the burnt chocolate hit him. "I just came from the schoolhouse and from what I could see there are more than enough sweets there already." He crossed the room and took her hand in his. "You didn't burn yourself, did you?" He was frowning and running his thumb over her palm.

Greta felt the color rise to her cheeks and she knew that she should pull her hand away. She was far too aware that the only burning going on at the moment was the heat she felt with Luke being so near. "Why did you come?" she asked, her voice catching in midsentence.

"Lydia sent me to tell you to be sure and remember to bring . . ." His eyes locked on hers and she realized that he had also lost his train of thought.

With a will of its own her head tilted up and her eyes fluttered shut as she fought to steady her breathing.

"Greta," he whispered, his lips so very close that she felt his breath tickle the strands of her hair that had worked their way free of her bun in the hot kitchen. "Do you think of me?"

"Constantly," she admitted. "And you?"

He chuckled. "I can't work. I can't sleep

for thinking about you — about us."

Greta fought a smile of pleasure and opened her eyes. "Me, too," she agreed.

But then all trace of his smile vanished and he stepped away. "It's important that you take plenty of time in this matter, Greta. You have suffered a great disappointment and . . ."

Oh, why did he have to spoil everything by bringing up the past? What was it about men that they had to always dwell on the realities of a matter? She turned away and began scrubbing the pan. "Of course, you're right," she said, her voice far too bright to be sincere. "Now what was it that Lydia did not want me to forget?"

"The extra cleaning rags," Luke said, his expression one of pure confusion at her sudden change in topic and conduct.

"They are there on the back porch. You can take them with you now."

"I had thought we might — that is, no one would think anything of it if you and I were to walk down to the schoolhouse together."

"And that's important to you, isn't it? That others not question your actions?"

He waited a long moment before he said anything, then quietly he said, "I thought such things were of concern to you, Greta."

Greta paused in her scrubbing, aware that

he had turned away and started for the door. She so wanted to stop him, to call him back, to rest her cheek against his chest and beg his forgiveness for her foul mood. "I'm sorry, Luke," she murmured but he was already gone, walking past the kitchen window with the basket of rags and an expression that looked like the coming of a storm.

"I'm sorry," she repeated and was struck by the difference in her apology to Luke from the ones she had offered to Josef over the years whenever something she said or did upset him. With Josef her apologies had been more a matter of habit — automatic in the knowledge that, whether she felt she had wronged him or not, this was the way to end whatever argument or disagreement they might be having. But with Luke the apology had come straight from her heart, from her understanding that her words had been hurtful and her change in attitude confusing for him.

She stood at the window with the scalded pot in one hand and a hunk of steel wool in the other and watched Luke until he was out of sight. And when she could no longer see him she felt such a sense of loss that she let the pot and steel wool fall from her slack hands as she ran from the house to catch up to him.

■ ■ ■ ■

"Luke! Wait!"

His heart hammered with relief as he turned to watch her run toward him. He savored the moment of Greta Goodloe running across the fallow field to him. The strings of her black bonnet had come undone and flew out behind her as she clutched at her bonnet with one hand and gathered the skirt of her dress and apron in the other to prevent herself from tripping. In his mind he was already years into the future and now she was wearing the white starched prayer covering of a married woman. She was running to him as his wife.

While he waited for her to catch up to him, he prayed that the dream of a union between them one day might be so and he vowed that soon he would find the right time to tell her everything that had happened in his past. Somehow in his heart he was sure that she would understand why he had made the choices he had made.

"Forgive me," she gasped when she reached him at last.

"There is nothing to forgive," he replied as he set down the basket and tried to tie the ribbons of her bonnet into a bow.

She looked up at him, the sun full on her face and he thought that he had never seen a woman more beautiful than Greta. "My fingers are too thick," he said huskily.

"I think your fingers are fine, although probably better for other tasks," she said as she took over the tying of the bow herself while he picked up the basket of rags and waited for her to finish. "I did not mean . . ."

"Sh-h-h. It's past."

She fell into step with him and side by side they walked the rest of the way to the schoolhouse. There seemed to be no need for further conversation and for that Luke was grateful, for he found that whenever he was around Greta he had trouble making his voice work or even coming up with the words he might say to her.

"Ah, here they are," Lydia said as soon as she spotted them. Her eyes flickered toward a small group of women that included Hilda Yoder who was scowling at them with disapproval.

"We have had to stop our work waiting for those clean rags, Luke Starns," Hilda chided. "What took you so long?"

Greta took the basket of cleaning rags from Luke and handed it to Lydia. "I ruined the cake and Luke was kind enough to help me clear the mess," she announced and in the background Luke heard several of the men groan.

"No matter," Lydia told her. "We have plenty." Then she clapped her hands together as she might if she were settling her students in for the day and began giving out assignments. "If you boys there would set up the ladders. The siding will need scraping before we can paint. Start on the north side and complete that so the men can begin the painting while you move on around the building." Next she pointed to the place where the desks had been set out into the yard along with the bookcases — empty of their books. "And Bettina, take your friends and the younger children and set to work polishing the desks and bookcases. Then you will need to dust every book, pound the chalk from the erasers and wash the chalkboard."

"Esther," Hilda called out. "Go with Bettina and the others."

Without question or comment the children ran to the shade of the large banyan tree and set to work, their excited chatter filling the heavy air that hung over the now empty school. Without the need for instruction, several of the men set to work climbing the ladders the boys had put in place and scraping the outer walls of the building while the women went inside to scrub the inner walls, wash the windows and polish the floor.

Around noon, Lydia sounded the bell and everyone gathered for the meal of cold cuts, cheeses, salads and desserts arrayed on boards set on sawhorses outside the schoolhouse. Like Sunday evening singings, frolics were acknowledged as occasions when males and females were allowed to socialize openly. With no comment from their elders, the older teens and young adults who were not yet married gathered in small groups to enjoy their lunch. Luke filled his plate and then took a seat on the ground next to Greta and Lydia.

He saw Hilda Yoder make some comment to Gertrude Hadwell as they looked his way. Both women nodded knowingly and smiled broadly at Lydia as they passed by on their way to sit with their husbands. Clearly they had no idea that it was Greta Goodloe being courted — not her sister. He glanced at Lydia and Greta and the three of them collapsed into laughter, drawing the attention of the two older women — as well as their frowns of censure. But Luke didn't care. For the first time in a very long time he felt a part of a community — a part of a family. Should he and Greta marry someday, then they would share many afternoons like this one with Lydia and Pleasant and Jeremiah and their children.

"Bettina is a good influence on Caleb Harnischer," Lydia said as she bit into a sandwich and nodded toward the teenagers. "He has become a far better student since taking up with her." She smiled as she glanced at Greta. "I have to say that I have noted some changes for the better in my sister recently, as well, Luke."

Luke sneaked a peek at Greta and grinned. Her cheeks were a rosy red and she was frowning. "In what ways would you say that she has changed, Lydia?"

"Oh, she is far more content these days and I hardly ever have to remind her to attend her chores and . . ."

"You have never had to remind me about chores, Lydia," Greta fumed.

Lydia lifted one eyebrow as she continued eating.

"At least not often. Most of the time you simply instruct out of habit, unaware that I have every intention of getting to whatever chore you may see."

Lydia turned her attention back to Luke. "You also seem in better spirits. With the disaster of the fire and your loss of business for those few weeks, it would be understandable for you to be a bit down in the dumps."

Now it was Luke's turn to flush. "My spirits have been uplifted by the kindness of my neighbors," he replied softly.

"That's it then?" Lydia pressed and he saw that she was fighting a smile.

"That's a good part of it. The rest I will keep to myself for now."

This brought a laugh from Lydia as she got to her feet and clapped her hands. "Back to work," she called and Greta was on her feet at once, collecting the used dishes from the others and organizing the washing up.

On her way back to the schoolhouse, Lydia paused and screened her eyes from the sun with her hand as she looked up at Luke. "I want to thank you."

"For?"

Lydia nodded toward Greta. "Whatever happens between you and my sister, you have seen her through a very difficult time. I would ask one more favor of you, though."

"Anything," Luke said and meant it. For when it came to Greta Goodloe he would happily move mountains if she needed him to do so.

"Do not hurt her," Lydia said. "If you find that you cannot love her — that she is not for you, then find a way to quit her so that she suffers no public humiliation."

"I have no intention of bringing Greta any pain at all if I can help it," Luke said quietly. "The truth is that you were wise to suggest we become better acquainted for I have come to see that . . ."

"Lydia Goodloe?" Hilda Yoder was standing by the entrance to the school, her hands on her ample hips and a scowl on her face as she watched Lydia and Luke closely. "The sun will not stay out forever," she reminded them. "And there is still a great deal of work to be done."

"Coming, Hilda," Lydia called, but before she turned away she looked up at Luke. "Just be very sure of your feelings, Luke."

"I will," he promised as she walked away. *I already am,* he thought.

As the work continued amid lively chatter and general high spirits, Luke was aware of the frequent lilt of Greta's laughter wafting out from the open windows to where he worked. He found it comforting somehow — the nearness of her.

All around him the men shared news they had heard about the state of the world outside Celery Fields. Mostly they talked about the man who had been elected President of the United States a year earlier. Franklin Delano Roosevelt was from a wealthy New York family and yet according to what several of the men had heard, he was focusing much of his attention on those that had suffered so much loss over the last few years. Luke heard the term *New Deal* and wondered why such a plan might be necessary. If neighbors worked together and took care of each other in hard times, as his neighbors had helped him after the fire and as they were all pitching in together now, there should be no need for a "new deal." He did not understand the ways of outsiders.

Above him the school bell clanged and he glanced up to see Greta balancing herself on the edge of the cupola as she reached to polish the large brass bell.

"Get down from there," he ordered, his fear that she might fall leaving a bitter taste in his mouth.

"Oh, Luke, don't worry. I have done this at least a dozen times — since Lydia and I were students here ourselves."

"You were smaller then and had more space to work and . . ."

She paused in her polishing and studied him. "Why, Luke Starns, I do believe that you are seriously concerned for my safety."

He saw a couple of the men working nearby glance his way, their interest suddenly on what was happening in their world

233

rather than the world of outsiders.

"As I would be concerned for anyone taking such a risk, Greta Goodloe," he replied, turning his attention back to his scraping. "But as you say, you have done this many times and after all I am new to all this."

He heard the men chuckle as they returned to their work and conversation. That's when he looked up at Greta, his eyes pleading with her to move to a safer position.

At first she gave him a teasing smile, but then as she read his expression, her eyes softened and she eased herself back inside the cupola. Seeing her on safer ground, he heaved a sigh of pure relief and found that he could breathe normally again. And once again it occured to him that breathing normally whenever he was anywhere near Greta — and sometimes even when he wasn't — was becoming more and more difficult.

As the day and the work progressed, Greta's thoughts seemed more fixed on the future than on the present — a future that it surprised her to realize definitely included Luke Starns. Surely it was far too soon for her to have such reflections that ran the gamut from what it would be like to be married to him to imagining sharing a home with him all the way to envisioning the children they would have. And yet she thought about all of those things and more. Where would they live? With more and more trucks and automobiles on the road would there be enough call for his blacksmithing skills and the use of the livery to sustain them? And what of Luke's family? He never spoke of them. All she knew was that his mother had died when he was young and his father and three brothers still lived in Ontario. The brothers were married and presumably had children.

If she married Luke she would be coming into a much larger family than the one that she and Lydia had in Florida. She imagined summer holidays spent in Canada away from the oppressive Florida heat. And of course, Luke's family would all come south to escape the harsh winters — many Amish families were doing that these days. They would hire a driver to bring them or come on the train or bus. This was allowed even though operating or owning any motorized vehicle of their own was not. She envisioned riding to Canada on the train with Luke after their wedding. Tradition had it that newly married Amish couples took several weeks to visit friends and family following the ceremony. Along the way they would receive gifts to help them set up their household. The idea made Greta smile as she completed the polishing of the bell and took her bucket and rags outside to start washing one of the school's tall windows. Slowly she polished the same area over and over again with the newspaper she'd soaked in a white vinegar solution once she'd cleaned away the surface dirt and grime.

"You're going to work your way right through the glass if you keep polishing that same spot," Luke teased. He had moved his ladder closer to where she was working and was painting the trim above her. "And I'm not sure I can mend a cut as easily as I removed that splinter."

Greta felt a rush of pleasure at his nearness. "Liddy likes for the windows to sparkle. She says the cleaner they are, the more light the children have to do their work by and that makes them better students."

"She certainly has a way with those youngsters," Luke agreed. He lowered his voice. "May I come by to see you tonight, Greta?"

But before Greta could reply, they were interrupted.

"You missed a spot way up there, Luke Starns," Esther Yoder shouted, coming alongside Greta before she could respond and pointing to a place that Luke hadn't gotten to yet. She giggled and glanced up at him. "Perhaps you need some help? I could hold the paint bucket while you reach those cornices."

Greta's mouth fell open. Esther Yoder was openly flirting with Luke when she knew — or thought she knew — that he was already courting Liddy. Of course he wasn't courting Liddy at all. He was courting her. Or at least that's what she'd thought until now when she looked up and saw Luke grinning down at Esther. He was giving the Yoder daughter that very same heart-stopping smile that he'd given Greta numerous times these last several days.

"Now, Esther, what would your mother say if I had you climb onto this ladder next to me?" he asked.

Esther's giggle turned into something more resembling a cackle. "My mother is not here, Luke. She's working inside."

The brazenness of Esther's invitation was downright shocking. The way Luke seemed to be eating it up was infuriating. "Luke," Greta said, intentionally keeping her tone sweet and adding a friendly smile for Esther's benefit, "if you've finished there, I think Lydia could use some help inside reaching the cobwebs that have gathered in the corners of that high ceiling." Greta fought to hold her composure despite her annoyance as she squinted up at him.

But when he turned the same smile that he'd offered Esther on her, Greta could tolerate no more. She gathered her bucket and newspaper and with a toss of her head went inside to find Lydia. "Never mind. I can ask one of the other men. I can see that you're still busy here." What could she have been thinking? Luke Starns was just like every other man she'd ever met — easily won over by sweet talk. Well, she would show him.

"Sister?" Lydia came clear across the room to meet her. "What has happened?"

"It's nothing," Greta assured her.

"But you're so flushed. Are you ill? Perhaps too much sun?" She pressed the back of her hand to Greta's cheek and it was all that Greta could do not to lean into the solace of her sister's touch. "Is it Luke?" Liddy asked, her voice barely audible in the din of chatter from the half-dozen other people busy working inside the small schoolroom.

Greta nodded. "He's no different than . . ."

"Now stop that," Lydia chided, still keeping her voice low. She glanced toward the window and evidently surmised the problem when she saw Esther still standing at the foot of Luke's ladder, gazing adoringly up at him and giggling at something he'd just said.

"First Josef and now Luke," Greta murmured. "Why does that woman dislike me so?"

"Be careful that you not suffer the sin of pride, sister," Lydia warned. "Besides, how can you think that Esther wishes to harm you by flirting with Luke? Let's remember that Josef has recently quit her, as well, and like it or not Luke Starns is one of the — if not the only — single man in the community that most women would set their eye on. Besides, wouldn't it make more sense if I were the one upset by Esther's actions?"

"*Yah,* I suppose, but . . ."

"I would remind you that, in all the years you spent with Josef, not once did I ever see you upset when some other girl caught his eye. But Luke Starns seems to have caused you great distress when I expect that all he was doing was being kind."

"He smiled at her," Greta argued.

Lydia laughed. "As he is prone to do these days — ever since he started coming around

239

and calling on you, I might add. God gave the man a wonderful smile, Greta. Would you deny him the use of it?"

"*Neh,* but . . ."

Lydia squeezed Greta's hand. It was a warning that almost came too late as Hilda Yoder was suddenly there beside them. "Is something wrong, Greta?" she asked.

"Nothing at all," Greta replied. "I've finished with the windows so Lydia and I were just going over the list of chores yet to be done." She turned to her sister. "The cobwebs, right? I'll get to them right away." She picked up a broom and wrapped the bristles with a clean rag.

"Oh, Greta, you are far too slight to reach the corners," Hilda huffed. She glanced toward the doorway. "You there, Luke Starns, come here and make yourself useful." She took the broom from Greta and handed it off to Luke. "Greta can show you where to reach." Then she smiled. "Or perhaps you would rather Lydia Goodloe instruct you?"

Greta almost laughed when she saw the sly look that Hilda gave Lydia. As if she knew a secret. But then the older woman's face collapsed into the more familiar grimace that she usually wore. "Esther," she called out when she spotted her daughter lingering near the doorway, her eyes on Luke. "I thought I sent you to make sure the young ones are doing a proper job polishing the desks. What are you doing in here?"

Esther mumbled an excuse and scurried back outside, her mother on her heels still lecturing her.

"That was close," Lydia said with a sigh. "Do you think you two can work together without causing trouble?"

"I . . ." Greta started to protest but Lydia was already halfway across the room, calling out to Caleb Harnischer to stop visiting with Bettina and get back to work.

"Want to show me where those cobwebs are hiding?" Luke asked as he scanned the rafters above them. "And while we're at it maybe you can tell me what just happened outside there? I thought we were . . ."

"We can talk about it tonight," Greta said primly as she led the way to the back of the room. "There," she pointed to a web that stretched across one corner.

Luke raised the broom and swiped at it until it was gone. The fact that he was smiling only irritated Greta more.

"Do you truly take such pleasure in removing cobwebs?" she asked as she continued to point and he continued to swipe, smiling the whole time.

"No. What I take pleasure in is knowing that even though you seem to be more than a little upset with me — for reasons I can't quite figure out — you're still going to let me come calling tonight."

"We have things to talk about that cannot be discussed here," she reminded him.

"Do I get a hint?"

"Just one — Esther Yoder."

"You think that . . ." he sputtered, drawing the attention of others.

"Hush," she hissed as she pointed to a far corner that forced him away from the prying eyes of the others.

"You can't be jealous." He had lowered his voice again and then he flashed that maddening grin of his. "Because that might mean that you care, Greta. It might mean that you care a great deal."

"And what if I do?"

He studied her for a long moment, his tone softening into something far more serious than the banter he'd been exchanging with her before. "I want you to be very sure," he said. "Because the fact is that I care about you — more than I would have thought possible."

She felt her mouth go slack in response to her surprise at such a declaration. "What are you saying?"

"I'm saying that when I come calling tonight, I'm hoping that we might do more than just talk," he said softly and as he then turned back to his work he was chuckling.

Suddenly Greta found that she was the one fighting a smile as she scanned the corners, praying to discover even more cobwebs so that she could stay close to Luke for the remainder of the afternoon. But in her mind she wasn't seeing the dark corners of the schoolhouse. She was seeing the two of them sitting together on the porch swing, in the shadows of the night, and Luke kissing her.

CHAPTER TWELVE

"You must be very tired, sister," Lydia commented later that evening after she had declared the work on the schoolhouse complete and sent everyone home.

"Not so very," Greta replied absently as she paced from the window of one of their two front rooms to the other across the hall.

"Are you expecting someone?" Lydia asked, not looking up from her mending.

"Luke mentioned that he might come by."

"And you agreed? I thought that you were annoyed with Luke," Lydia said.

Greta plopped down in the upholstered chair on the other side of the fireplace that they used to heat the front rooms on those rare days when the Florida weather turned chilly. "Oh, Liddy, I don't know what I feel for him. I keep telling myself that it's only been a few weeks. How is it possible that in such a short time I might have come to . . ." She waved her hands in frustration then clasped them tightly around her knees as if it were necessary for her to hold herself together. "To what? I have no understanding of my feelings when it comes to that man but these last few days . . ."

"Have you considered the idea that perhaps you are in love with Luke Starns?" Lydia said, her voice as calm as if she had simply asked Greta if she intended to make chicken or beef for their supper.

"How could I love him?" Greta protested. "Surely it's far too soon."

"God does not work on our timetables, sister," Lydia reminded her. "If it is His will for you and Luke to be together, then why wait?"

"But how can I be certain?" Greta moaned.

Lydia lightly tapped the place on her chest where her heart beat. "You must pray for guidance and when the time is right then you will know it here."

They both looked up at the sounds of footsteps on the porch. After a moment the swing creaked and Lydia folded her mending. "It has been a long but fruitful day and I find that I am very tired, Greta." She kissed her sister's forehead as she passed her on the way to her room. "Let God guide you," she said softly.

"Easy for you to say," Greta mumbled as she remained sitting in the chair by the unlit fireplace. Then as she had done her whole life, she followed her sister's advice. She squeezed her eyes closed and prayed silently.

After a long moment she heard Luke quietly calling to her through the open window. "Greta, will you not come out?"

"*Yah,* coming."

Slowly she walked to the door and out onto the porch where she was surprised to see Luke standing rather than sitting on the swing. He took a step toward her and held out his arms and she did not hesitate to walk directly into his embrace.

"I am sorry for upsetting you earlier today," he said as he folded his arms around her, creating a kind of safe cocoon that Greta found she never wanted to leave.

Was this feeling of coming home God's answer? Was He showing her that Luke was the man she would spend her life with? Lydia had advised prayer and then listening to her heart, and while her prayer had been brief and interrupted by Luke's presence, there was no denying what her heart was telling her in this moment. "It's so late," she murmured. "I thought you might be too weary."

"Come and sit with me. I want to tell you

something," Luke said as he led the way back to the swing.

He sounded so very serious that Greta feared that he might have decided to quit her as Josef had done. But if that were the case, would he have come at all? And would he now be holding both her hands between his own as he sat forward on the swing so that he could face her?

The lamp from the front room cast its glow on her features while Luke's face remained in shadow. "What is it?" she asked and the tremor in her voice gave away her nervousness.

He cleared his throat, revealing his own unease. "I know that the time we have spent together has not been long," he began. "And it would be wrong of me to ask this without acknowledging that."

He sounded as if he were delivering a speech, one he had practiced many times.

Greta's heart sank.

"But," he continued after drawing in a deep breath, "I have come to a decision."

"I see," Greta whispered. "Perhaps Lydia should be present for this?"

He seemed surprised by the suggestion. "Why would . . ."

"If you are quitting me, then Lydia must know for others will surely . . ."

"I am not quitting you, Greta. I love you. I am asking you to — when you are ready and certain — to become my wife."

Greta's mouth fell open but no sound came out so Luke rushed forward. "As I have said, I realize that our time together has been brief and you may not yet be ready to make such a decision — such a commitment. But I have prayed much on this matter and I truly believe that God is leading me in this. You should take the time you need — days, weeks, even months if necessary — to be very certain of your answer. I will wait. For I know without a doubt that you are the reason I came to Celery Fields. God was leading me to you and even if you see matters otherwise and refuse me, then . . ."

Greta laid her finger on his lips to quiet his ramblings. "I accept," she said. "I would marry you, Luke Starns." She slipped her hands from his and cupped the smooth skin of his jaw. "I will be your wife."

"You are certain?"

Greta laughed. "Are you?"

"Yah," he replied, his voice husky as he moved closer. "I am very, very certain."

In the past he had kissed her or she had kissed him but this time their kiss was shared, each meeting the other's lips with all the fervor of the decision they had just made. Greta's heart sang with the pure joy of realizing that everything she had ever dreamed of for herself would now be true, including a life with a man who truly cared for her — loved her. She and Luke would marry and settle together in a home of their own where they would raise a family and live — God willing — many years together. She thought that her heart might fly right out of her body, so truly happy was she.

But when Luke pulled away from the kiss, he seemed once again to be struggling to find the words he wanted to say to her.

"I love you, Luke," she said softly. She had never uttered those words before and yet they seemed so very right and true now. "I have never found a way to speak those words with — anyone else, but I find them coming so easily now. I love you with all my heart."

"There are things you must yet know," Luke said and she did not like the way his voice had taken on a tone of warning. "If we are to be together then you must know everything about my past about my family . . ."

"Sh-h-h," she whispered. "There will be time enough for us to each learn all that has brought each of us to this moment. Whatever is past should remain there. I want only for us to look ahead. Oh, Luke, we are going to be so very happy. Please don't spoil this moment with worries about the past."

"But it is only right that . . ."

"Whatever it is that you are burdened with from your days in Ontario, it does not matter. If you love me, then that is everything I need. We will build a life — here." He said nothing and as they sat in silence for several long minutes Greta could not quell her fears. "Luke? Tell me that you are not having doubts."

Luke pulled her closer and kissed her forehead. "No doubts. Never any doubts."

Greta settled against him. "Then you will go and see Levi Harnischer first thing tomorrow?" Levi was the deacon of their congregation and as such it was his role to receive the man's request to wed and then to visit the family of the proposed bride to be sure that her parents — or in Greta's case, Lydia — and the bride were in agreement.

"Are you saying that you do not wish to wait — to be certain?"

"I am already certain." She giggled happily. "Levi will be surprised that it is me you wish to marry," she warned. "Everyone thinks that you and Lydia . . ."

Luke chuckled as he sat back and pulled her to him, his arm resting around her shoulders. "*Yah,* no doubt there will be many surprised people." He sighed with pleasure and gently rocked the swing.

Greta thought she had never before felt so protected nor so certain of what lay ahead for her. "Let's go tell Lydia," she suggested.

"It is late and she will be sleeping. Besides, we have much we need to discuss before we share our news with others — even with Lydia."

"But she will know something has changed the minute she sees my face for I will not be able to contain my happiness, Luke." She grabbed his hand and pulled him to his feet. "Come on. We can talk about whatever serious matters you think we must discuss tomorrow."

"Greta, you don't understand. Please, you must listen to . . ."

"Liddy!" she shouted, allowing the screen door to slam with a bang behind them as she and Luke entered the house.

As Greta had expected, Lydia came running from her room, wrapping her shawl around her, her bare feet padding on the wood floors. "What's happened now?" she asked and then froze in the archway that led from the front room to the bedrooms when she saw Luke standing next to Greta.

"God has spoken," Greta announced.

"Sister!" With a single word Lydia warned against any blasphemy but then she looked from Greta to Luke and back again. "You are to marry?"

"We are," Luke replied, "with your agreement."

"Luke is going to see Levi tomorrow morning first thing," Greta gushed. "And then Levi will come here tomorrow evening and then . . . Oh, Liddy, we have so much to do. Do you think we should tell Pleasant? I mean she is family, as well, and . . ."

"It's to be soon then?" For the first time Lydia seemed to have some concern. "The wedding?"

"Why would we wait?" Greta asked, fighting to keep her tone light in the face of her sister's unexpected doubt.

But Luke placed his hand on her shoulder. "Lydia is right to question the suddenness of our decision, Greta." He stepped forward and faced Lydia directly. "I can only tell you, Lydia Goodloe, that in a very short time I have come to love your sister more than I would have thought myself capable of loving anyone. I find that there is hardly an hour that passes when she is not in my thoughts and I promise you that I will do everything I can to see that she is well cared for and happy."

Greta watched as Lydia worried her lower lip, a sure sign that she was not completely convinced. "This was your idea, Liddy," she reminded her. "It has worked out as you prayed. Can you not be happy for us?"

Lydia looked from Greta to Luke and then she walked forward, extending one hand to each of them until the trio had formed a little circle there in the front room. "I am happy for you, Greta. And as for you, Luke, it will be good to have a brother."

"And I will have a sister," he replied.

"We must write to your father and brothers at once," Greta said, pulling free of the circle as she hurried to the desk and pulled out writing paper and a pen.

"There will be time enough for that," Lydia said. "Right now, we should all get some rest."

"Your sister is right, Greta," Luke said as he gently relieved her of the pen and placed it back on the desk. "I will speak to Levi tomorrow — today," he added as they all glanced at the tall clock standing in the front hallway that was just striking midnight. "*Guten nacht,* Lydia."

"*Guten nacht,* Luke," Lydia replied as she drew her shawl around her and headed back down the hall. "Do not be out there seeing Luke off for too long, sister," she warned, but there was a lilt to her voice that told Greta that Lydia did not really care if the happy couple stayed on the porch until dawn.

As soon as Liddy's door closed with a soft click, Greta gave a soft cry of pure joy and flung herself into Luke's arms. "I love you. I love you. I love you," she said, punctuating each declaration with a kiss and filled with the joy of knowing without a doubt that she had discerned God's plan for her life — and this time she had gotten it right.

In the face of Greta's euphoria, Luke decided to postpone the conversation he knew they would need to have about his past. Surely he would be able to make her understand why he had left his home in Ontario to move to Celery Fields. Surely she would see that he had really had no choice. And in the meantime it gave him great pleasure to see her so happy. So early the following morning he drove out to the Harnischer farm and stood in the barn, speaking with Levi Harnischer — the deacon of their congregation. As Luke had expected, Levi Harnischer was taken aback when he heard of Luke's intention to marry Greta.

"You are already the nervous bride-groom," Levi teased. "You mean to say that it is Lydia Goodloe that . . ."

"I have not mistaken my words, Levi. It is Greta Goodloe whom I wish to wed," Luke said firmly. Then he told Levi how Lydia had come up with the plan to allow Greta and Luke the time they might need to get better acquainted while everyone in Celery Fields thought that Lydia was the object of his affections. "After Josef Bontrager quit Greta, I believe that Lydia was somewhat relieved but that she also felt an urgency to take some action to turn her sister's head in a new direction. She thought that Josef might realize his mistake and try to win Greta back."

"As he has," Levi noted. "So, it is Lydia who set this plan in place?"

"*Yah.* But she did so with Greta's full agreement."

"And you also agreed?"

"Not at first. But then I prayed on the matter and it seemed that with Josef quitting Greta perhaps there was a message in the timing of things. I cannot deny that when I first came to Celery Fields I was drawn to Greta, but she was with Josef and so I turned my attention to Lydia."

"And she rejected you?"

"She did, as she seems inclined to reject the very notion of marriage for her at all. You should understand that Lydia was quite worried about Greta. She made it clear that she did not necessarily expect the match between Greta and me to be one of true love, but rather one in which her sister could achieve the life that she had always aspired to live."

"And do you love her — Greta?"

"More than I would have thought possible."

"And what of her feelings for you?"

"She has said that she loves me in return." *Repeatedly,* Luke thought, and could not seem to hide the smile that tugged at the corners of his mouth.

"And all of this has come to pass in what — a matter of a few weeks?"

"A little longer than that," Luke protested but he knew that he was splitting hairs. It had been a courtship of what some would see as a shockingly short duration. "I am not some teenager just coming from his *Rumspringa,* Levi. And Greta herself is past her twentieth birthday already."

Levi stroked his beard, still dark like his hair but with hints of gray. "When is this marriage to take place?"

"As soon as possible." Luke saw the

startled glance that Levi gave him and hastened to add, "We are both anxious to begin our life together."

"I see. You are asking me then to serve as the *Schtecklimann* — the go-between for brokering this marriage?"

"We wish to do everything properly," Luke said, "although Greta — and Lydia — have already given their consent. But in the absence of living parents, I had thought that you might call on Lydia and Greta for their assurance that they are in agreement with this plan. Perhaps their half sister Pleasant should be there, as well?"

"I would think so. Pleasant was like a mother to both those girls for some years." He finished tossing clean hay onto the floor of the stable stalls and turned to face Luke. "All right, I will call on the sisters tomorrow and unless there is something that would prevent this union, I will report to Bishop Troyer and he can publish your intent at our next service."

"Das ist gut." Luke tried hard to ignore the dread he felt at the deacon's words about something preventing the union. Once again, he vowed to himself and God that he would tell Greta the story of his past the very next day.

But as they sat together on her front porch

the following evening with a steady rain falling, Greta was anxious to tell him every last detail of the meeting that she and Lydia and Pleasant had had with Levi earlier that night. By tradition, the deacon had arrived after dark. "I suppose that's in case the parents — or in this case, Lydia — deny permission. That way no one loses face since presumably no one else is aware of the courtship — although that's unlikely in a place as small as Celery Fields." She was babbling, but it was born of her excitement and happiness so she hurried on to tell him the rest. "It was all so very serious," she said with a mock grimace. "As if Levi needed to assure himself that I — that we — knew what we were doing."

"He was just doing his job as *Schtecklimann*," Luke reminded her. "It's all part of the tradition."

"I know. It's meaningless — no more than a formality passed down through the generations. I mean what was he going to do? Tell me not to marry you?"

"That would not be his place."

"Anyway, once he had gone through the ritual and Lydia and Pleasant had assured him that they approved, he did seem genuinely happy for us. Oh, Luke, we have so much planning to do. I mean if our intent is to be published this next Sunday, there is no time to waste."

Luke chuckled and stretched his arm across the back of the swing. She leaned her head against his shoulder. "I am pretty sure that Bishop Troyer and the others are well practiced at this, Greta."

"I'm not talking about the announcement itself — there's the ceremony to plan. We'll need to allow time for friends and relatives from out-of-town to arrive. But even so, we need to set a date for just a few weeks from now if we are to make the journey north to visit friends and family and still be back in time for the harvest season."

In the days when they were first getting to know one another, Luke had explained to her how he was busiest during the planting and harvest seasons. Those were the times when the horseshoes and equipment his neighbors used for plowing and harvesting their crops were more likely to need a repair. This year, whatever business he could take in during the harvest season would be especially important since the fire that had destroyed Luke's business had come at the very height of the planting season, severely limiting his ability to serve his customers.

Greta continued to chatter on about plans for the ceremony and the meal that would follow, but Luke listened only to the lilt of her voice so filled with joy and excitement. He felt such power in realizing that he was the cause of her elation. He was relishing the picture she painted with her planning right up until the moment when she began speaking about their wedding trip.

"Do you honestly think that we can travel all the way to Canada and still be back in time?" she asked. "How long does the train take? And what of the cost?"

"Canada?"

"To see your family, of course. Unless you think they might be able to come here for the ceremony. But you mentioned that your father's health has not been good so perhaps it's best if we go there. I can't wait to meet your father and brothers. Do you think they'll like me? And what about the wives?"

Luke swallowed. The time had come. In truth the time had passed when he should have told Greta exactly why he had left Canada and moved to Celery Fields. "Greta, we cannot include my family in this."

"Why on earth not?" She smiled uncertainly. "Oh, do they do things differently there? I mean is the tradition of a wedding trip not part of . . ."

Luke closed his eyes against the understanding that the moment he had dreaded for days was at hand. He had allowed himself to be swayed by Greta's assurances that there was nothing he could tell her that could possibly change her feelings for him. Yet all the while he had known that indeed there was something.

"Listen to me," he said sternly. "When I was living in Canada, Greta, there was a woman — two women . . ." He felt Greta stiffen as if she were preparing herself for bad news. "I had passed my *Rumspringa* — my running around time — and my *Dat* was urging me to settle down. All my brothers were married already with families of their own and my father was getting along in years. He was already in poor health and it was important to him to see us all settled. He had promised my mother."

"Did you love these women?" Her voice was dull and carried no hint of her usual enthusiasm.

"Not really — I never thought about the need for love to be a part of choosing a wife, Greta. It was something to be done at a certain stage of life. Admittedly I thought that perhaps the younger one . . . that in time . . ."

"What happened?"

"The young woman's father had other

ideas. Like Laban with Jacob, he wanted his elder daughter to marry first."

"These were sisters?"

"Yah."

"Like Lydia and me." Her voice was thin as if her vocal cords were stretched too tight and she did not look at him.

"In some ways, yes. Certainly the elder one was like Lydia in that she had made up her mind that she would not marry. But her father had other ideas and like the story of Laban and his daughters, he was intent on seeing her married."

"But you and the younger sister . . ."

"There was nothing there, either," Luke said softly. "I see that now. At the time I thought that she and I could make a life but that was all there was to it. It was plain that she hoped her sister would agree to their father's plan."

Greta edged away from him on the pretense of reaching for a dry leaf that had blown onto the porch.

Luke felt such a sense of panic that it was all he could do not to grab her by the shoulders and force her to face him — to hear him out. "Greta, I am asking you to believe me when I say that even then — before I ever knew you existed — I did not feel for her anything close to what I feel whenever I look at you."

"Did you kiss her?"

"No. Her father would not permit the courtship."

"But you would have?"

"I don't know. I suppose. That's not the point, Greta. The point is that I did not marry either of them."

"If your only purpose was to seek a wife, why not the elder one?"

Luke had never imagined that this would be so very difficult. "Because I understood that marrying was not something that she wanted. Unfortunately her father would not listen to reason. In the end there was an accident involving the elder sister. She did not survive."

"Oh, Luke, how horrible. But then the father — surely he would want his younger daughter — I mean, in time . . ."

Luke shook his head. "There is more," he said, his throat closing around the words making it nearly impossible for him to speak.

"That's enough," Greta said softly as she sat forward, pulling away from him and folding her arms protectively over her chest. "I don't need to know anything more. I am sorry for the loss of this woman and for what her family must have suffered but,

Luke, this is our time — our happy time." She turned to him and in the lamplight he saw her eyes go wide with pleading. "Can we not just let the past go?"

And once again, against his better judgment, Luke agreed. But as she settled back into the curve of his arm and he rested his cheek on her fair hair, he realized that he had allowed himself to set aside his past. A past he had hoped to put behind him by coming to Celery Fields. But that was not possible — not now. Before their intent to wed was published, he had to find a time to tell Lydia the whole story. If Lydia still accepted him as a proper husband for Greta in spite of his past, then they would go forward. If not, he would seek the promise of Levi and Bishop Troyer to say nothing of the plan to wed Greta so that she would not have to suffer the pity of others yet again. Then he would make Greta hear him out so that she would understand once and for all why he would not tarnish her good name with his past and why he would leave Celery Fields for good.

CHAPTER THIRTEEN

On Monday evening before the Sunday that the union between Luke and Greta was to be published at services, Lydia and Greta were at supper discussing the plans for the wedding when there was a knock at the front door.

"That will be Luke," Lydia said. "He has asked to speak with me privately."

Before Greta could question her, Lydia went to the door and Greta could not have been more surprised to hear her sister exclaim, "Why, Josef Bontrager, you're back from your travels. Come in and share our supper."

Greta took that as her cue to set another place at the small kitchen table. She offered up a quick prayer to keep her high spirits and excitement about the coming wedding in check so as not to wound Josef. "Hello, Josef," she said when he entered the kitchen. "Did you have a good trip?"

She waited until he sat down and then filled his glass with sweet tea before taking her own place next to him and offering him a helping of the meat loaf and mashed potatoes that she had made. The sisters sat in silence while Josef bowed his head in a brief prayer.

"I was not traveling for pleasure," Josef stated as if she had somehow accused him of frivolity. He snapped open his napkin and tucked it into the neck of his shirt.

"Business then," Lydia said and offered him the bread.

He helped himself to two thick slices and reached for the butter. "I am afraid that I have returned with some news, Greta. News that will no doubt wound you in the telling but that will nevertheless save you from making a mistake that could . . ."

Greta set aside her fork and folded her hands in her lap. She was all too familiar with this side of Josef. He liked to deliver bad news preceded by a lecture. "Just tell us what you came to say, Josef."

He ignored her request and continued to set the stage for his news. "It would seem that things between you and the blacksmith have moved forward at a faster pace than I would have hoped, Greta."

"What makes you say such a thing?" Greta

asked, casting a worried look at Lydia.

"My Uncle Cyrus went to see Levi Harnischer the other evening but he was away. Hannah said he had come to town. My uncle saw Levi's buggy parked outside your house and as the deacon was leaving Cyrus heard him say that he would tell the bishop to publish the news."

"Your uncle spied on us," Greta said flatly, not in the least surprised that Cyrus Bontrager would stoop to such tactics.

"Oh, Josef," Lydia entreated, "you really must accept that Greta has . . ."

"So now you know the news. It's true, Josef. Bishop Troyer will publish our intent to wed at services next Sunday."

"You cannot allow this," Josef exclaimed, turning to Lydia.

"It is not for you to decide . . ." Lydia protested but Greta interrupted her.

"Let him say what he has come to say, Liddy." Her fists were clenched now and she was having trouble breathing. The panic she had felt that day weeks earlier when Josef had quit her was back. Only this time it was ten times worse. She focused all of her attention on Josef. "Just tell us why you have come here, Josef."

Josef helped himself to the meatloaf and mashed potatoes that Greta had prepared for her supper with Lydia. "Luke Starns is under the *Bann,*" he said as he scooped food onto his plate without looking at either sister.

Lydia glanced at Greta and smiled uncertainly. Greta focused all of her attention on her plate.

"He was excommunicated by his church in Ontario," Josef continued, stuffing his mouth with the food as if he had not eaten in days. "And that is why he left there and started up his business here. That is also why he had no letter from his bishop to present when he joined our congregation. He has deceived you, Greta. He has deceived all of us, allowing us to do business with him and welcome him into the fold of our community when all along he knew . . ."

"Surely there is some explanation," Lydia challenged. "What were the circumstances?"

"I will say only that the circumstances were not dissimilar to the situation here in that they involved two sisters." He paused to take a long drink of his tea before adding, "One of them ended up dead and the circumstances surrounding that death were at the very root of Luke's being cast out."

"You are accusing Luke of murder?" Greta was outraged.

"I am not accusing Luke of anything. He

stands accused by his own congregation and shunned by his own family. Some say her death was an accident but, by and large, most believe that she died by her own hand. All are convinced that she died of a broken heart when Luke rejected her."

"Without knowing all of the circumstances, you cannot hold him responsible for a decision made by another," Lydia argued but her voice shook and Greta saw that she had been completely unnerved by Josef's news.

Josef took a bite of his bread — bread that Greta wanted to rip from his hand. How could he drop such news on them and go on calmly eating his supper? He was enjoying this. She wanted to tell him that she already knew about the sisters in Ontario, that she already knew that the elder one had died — although it was true that Luke had failed to tell her the details. On the other hand, she had not asked — had not wanted to know of anything so sad in the face of her own joy.

"Liddy is right," she argued, determined to defend Luke. "If this woman did not die by his actions, then of what could he be accused?"

"Arrogance in his refusal to accept the accusation made by the woman's father and to make any amends or seek any forgiveness." He sopped up the last of the sauce on his plate with the crust of bread. "I have already spoken to Bishop Troyer and presented him with a letter that the bishop in Ontario asked me to bring back with me. A letter insisting that our congregation uphold the *Bann* on Luke or risk creating disunity within the larger church."

"Why have you done this?" Greta whispered, her hands shaking so hard now that all she could do to still them was to knit her fingers together.

For the first time since his arrival, Josef turned all of his attention to her. He set his fork on the plate and pulled the napkin from his shirt, wiping his mouth with it before explaining. "Can you not see that I did it for you, Greta? It was for you that I left my farm with the fields barely plowed and traveled to Canada. It was for you that I sought to learn the truth about this man — to save you from possibly becoming his next victim. We have long known that the circumstances that brought Luke here were never fully revealed and . . ."

"You did not do any of this for me, Josef Bontrager. You did it for you — out of your sense of wounded pride that I had moved forward with my life after you quit me."

"I had hoped, of course, that you and I could find our way back to each other — that is still my hope. But even in the absence of that I could not allow . . ."

A strength born of outrage roiled through Greta, bringing her to her feet. He could not *allow*? He was not her father or brother and certainly not her husband. He had no right to decide what was best for her. "I must go," she said tightly even as she took down her bonnet and tied it in place.

"Greta, wait," Lydia called after her.

But Greta was already halfway across the yard that separated their house from Luke's shop. He would still be working and not yet aware of the doom that Josef Bontrager had brought back with him from his trip to Ontario. For the moment she had every reason to believe that Luke was still as happy and excited about their future as she had been just before Josef showed up on their doorstep.

She knew she was too late the minute she rounded the corner of the shop and saw Levi Harnischer's buggy parked outside. Levi rarely came to town on a weekday unless he had business to attend to in his role as deacon of their congregation. And although there was the possibility that he had come to town on other business, that was

271

unlikely at this late hour. Greta slowed her step as she edged her way toward the open double doors. She heard the murmur of male voices, surprisingly calm if the conversation was what she thought it must be.

She peered around the frame of the door and saw Luke sitting on the chair he had offered her that day that now seemed so very long ago. He was holding a paper while Levi and Bishop Troyer stood quietly by. He handed the letter back to the bishop and stood up. Although she could not make out his words without moving further inside the shop and revealing her presence, Greta could tell by his gestures that Luke was telling the two church elders the story.

It was a story that he had tried to tell her, she realized. They were to be married and she understood now that before the news was made public he had wanted to make sure that she knew about his past — all of it. She realized that in trying to tell her about the sisters, he had wanted to see if perhaps she would be willing to forgive him. Now the entire business would be made public — as was right, she understood. But allowing everyone to learn of Luke's past could destroy their happiness.

For if the people of Celery Fields knew that he had left Canada under the *Bann,* then they would have had no choice but to honor that. No one in Celery Fields could do business with Luke or invite him to join them in their homes or sit down for a meal with him. And what was she to do? She who loved him more than she had ever thought she could love a man?

She jumped as she felt a hand on her shoulder and turned to find Lydia standing next to her.

"Come home, sister," Lydia pleaded. "It is out of our hands now."

"Josef?"

"I sent him home."

Greta nodded and gave herself over to her sister's steadfast strength and comfort as she had all her life — as she no doubt would need to for the remainder of her days. Once again there would be no publication of her coming wedding at services, no happy exclamations of surprise from the other women, no moments of doubt as others tried to decide if this was good news or if they should pity Lydia. There would be instead the shocking revelation that this man, that all of Celery Fields had taken into their homes and hearts, had deceived them all by keeping a secret that in their world was unforgivable.

■ ■ ■ ■

Luke was trying to explain the circumstances alluded to in his former bishop's letter when he saw a flash of movement at the door of his shop. *Greta.* There was no reason she would have come to him at this time of day. They had made plans for him to come to the house after dark, where they would sit together as they had through so many evenings now planning their future. No, Bontrager had gotten to her. He must have gone straight there after delivering the letter to Bishop Troyer.

Every fiber of his being wanted to go to her, to hold her and tell her that they would find their way through this. But then he saw Lydia take Greta away and he knew that to involve her in any way was to do her irreparable harm. She would be forgiven for associating with him while everyone assumed that she had no knowledge of his past, but if she had anything to do with him now . . .

"Luke?" Levi placed a hand on his shoulder.

From the moment the bishop and Levi had entered his shop, the two men had talked to him in tones that spoke of the

274

seriousness of the situation and yet their kindness toward him was evident. He understood that they hoped — as had his family and friends back in Ontario — to find a way to resolve things so that he could be reinstated into the good graces of the church.

"I will seek the congregation's forgiveness for not revealing my past," Luke said.

There was a silence that Bishop Troyer and Levi filled with the exchange of worried looks. "I'm afraid, Luke, that seeking our forgiveness will not be enough. You must resolve this business with your former congregation in Ontario."

"Don't you think I tried to do that?" Luke said. "But the deacon there is the woman's father and in his understandable grief he would not hear of anything less than my admission that I had caused her to take her life. It was a lie, Bishop Troyer. And to my dying day I will never believe that Dorie took her own life."

"That is the story," Levi said, pointing to the paper they had shown Luke.

"That is *their* story. Dorie often walked along the river when she needed to think or work something out. The rains had made the path slippery and soggy. I believe that the bank gave way and she was washed into the swift current."

"And that may have been the way of it," Josef Bontrager announced, stepping out from the shadows at the back of the shop and coming forward. "But the fact remains, Luke Starns, that this woman felt the need to think on that day because you had rejected her. She would not have been there had it not been for your cruelty in quitting her for her sister."

Luke clenched his fists at his sides and forced his voice to remain calm. "Everyone knew that it was Dorie's father who wanted the match between us. Dorie had stated her intention to remain unwed, but her father would not hear of it. What Dorie overheard that day was her father offering to pay me in land and cash if I would agree to marry her."

"How can you possibly know what this woman overheard?" Josef sneered.

"Because I spoke with her later that same day and she told me. I asked her to come with me so that together we could talk with her father but she refused, saying that she needed some time to think. That was the last that I or anyone else saw of her until her body was found the following morning."

"So you say."

"So says the entire congregation," Luke

replied. "Every person voted in favor of my reinstatement save that Dorie's father. As you are well aware the vote must be unanimous and so I was excommunicated. I lost everything."

"But surely you can recognize that the disunity your actions created within the community . . ."

"What actions?" Luke challenged. "Somebody tell me what I did wrong and I will own it, but I cannot admit to something that I did not do nor can I seek forgiveness if I have no knowledge of what the accusations are."

Levi held up the letter. "You were charged with arrogance, Luke."

Luke drew in a breath to steady himself. It was all happening again. "Because I would not admit to something I did not do, I was accused of arrogance. Was I to surrender to the lie that I had caused the woman to take her life when it was not true and everyone knew that?"

"There is, in the *Ordnung,* the requirement that we be submissive to the greater good of the community," Josef reminded him.

"I . . ." Luke threw up his hands in a gesture of surrender. What was the point? In trying to defend himself he could be accused of arrogance again for in their faith a man did not put himself above the whole — the community. "What do you wish me to do?" he asked the bishop, turning his back on Josef and any more pronouncements that he might decide to make.

"On Sunday following the service we will publicize this entire matter to the congregation. I will advise that we take the next two weeks to pray for guidance and at the following service I will bring my recommendation for their vote. Until then we will abide by the situation as it is stated in this letter. And," he added, turning to face Josef directly, "we will not speak of this matter to anyone outside this building until that is all in place."

"But at the very least for those two weeks, Luke Starns, you will be . . ."

"Meidung," Luke murmured. "Shunned."

Levi placed his hand on Luke's forearm. "Of course, you may continue to conduct your business and reside in the community. However . . ."

"I know how this works, Levi," Luke said gently for he understood that the other man was only trying to be as clear as possible without being cruel. "I endured that punishment for months before I decided to leave Ontario and come here. To this day I have not heard from my father or brothers, although I write to them regularly."

Bishop Troyer grasped Luke's shoulder briefly and then walked away. "I find that I am quite weary, Levi," he said. "Would you be so kind as to drive me home?"

"Yah," Levi murmured. "Coming, Josef?" he asked but Luke gratefully understood that this was not a question but an instruction to the man who had managed to destroy any chance Luke might have had for happiness.

"Greta will try and see you," Josef said in a low voice as he hesitated before following the others outside. "I will do my best to console her but . . ."

Luke stood toe to toe with the shorter, heavier man. "You stay away from her," he ordered.

"Or what?" Josef challenged but a thin line of sweat trickled down his temples and Luke saw that the man was afraid of him.

Luke stepped away, effectively releasing Josef without ever having touched him. "Just stay away until this is settled. She will need time."

Josef looked at him, his eyes squinting with curiosity. "You would give up so easily?"

"I would protect the woman I love from

gossip and scandal," Luke replied and turned back to his work, taking out all his frustration at this latest turn of events by pounding out a hot piece of iron on the anvil. Behind him he heard Josef's footsteps moving quickly away.

When all three men were gone, Luke moved to the small window and stood for a long time, staring out at the deserted street. The sun was almost set now and he knew that, in houses all around Celery Fields, families would be gathering for their evening prayers.

He took off his leather apron and hung it on the hook then walked outside and down the street toward the old Obermeier house at the far end of town. He had bought the property earlier that week from Pleasant. It had been the home of her first husband and the place where his four children had been born. It had been Pleasant's home after his death while she ran the bakery and raised the children until Jeremiah Troyer came to town. For the last couple years, it had sat vacant and neglected and Pleasant had been happy to hear that Luke wanted to live there.

"Alone?" she had asked with a twinkle in her eye.

"For now," he had replied and been unable to stifle the half smile that tugged at his mouth whenever he thought about the life he was going to build with Greta.

He had asked that Pleasant not speak of the transaction to anyone else. "The house is to be a gift," he told her, knowing that he needn't say more, for having been with Lydia and Greta when Levi called to seek their approval of Luke's proposal, Pleasant now knew the whole story.

In preparation for getting the house refurbished and ready for Greta, he had gathered all of the supplies he would need and stored them in the abandoned chicken coop behind the house. His plan had been that once the announcement of their upcoming wedding had been publicized at services, he would spend every spare hour working to ready the house for their wedding night.

Now it hardly mattered when he worked on the property. Now there was no longer any reason to keep the surprise for Greta. For now there would be no wedding, no house for them to share, no future with the only woman he had ever truly loved. He had told Bontrager that he wanted to protect Greta from gossip and scandal. But in truth, by not admitting to his past when he had first come to Celery Fields, by not insisting that she hear him out — all of it — before she agreed to marry him, he had brought her the very pain that he had sought to avoid.

Luke climbed the front steps and sat down on the weather-warped boards of the porch. He buried his face in his hands as he prayed for God's guidance. And when he looked up and looked over the town that he had come to think of as home, he saw one lamp burning. It stood where it had stood every night since he and Greta Goodloe had first started keeping company and to his eyes it was like a beacon drawing him to her.

Greta did not know whether or not he would come but she was determined to stay on the porch swing until dawn in case he did. Lydia had refused to make any comment on the story that Josef brought them about Luke or on the few details that Greta was able to offer based on her conversations with Luke.

"I will pray on the matter," she had said. "I suggest you do the same. There must be some explanation beyond what Josef has been able to uncover," she had added as she went to her room, her Bible grasped firmly in her hands.

It occurred to Greta that Lydia had come to care for Luke a great deal — and the feeling was reciprocated. Oh, it was nothing remotely romantic. The two of them interacted as if they were already family — favorite cousins or sometimes even sister and brother. Lately when Luke came calling, Lydia would join them on the porch for part of the evening and the conversation would often turn to the difficulties each faced at work. Enrollment at the school was down now that so many families had moved north and Lydia worried that the elders might be forced to close the school altogether. Meanwhile Luke's non-Amish customers — who were an important part of his business — had fallen on hard times. Many had lost their jobs or businesses and could not afford his services.

Greta preferred to focus her attention on happier topics but she was glad that Lydia took an interest in Luke's business, as he did in her teaching. One day he had even gone to the school to speak to the students about the work he did. That evening Lydia had come home beaming and at supper she had announced to Greta that one day Luke was going to make a fine father. "And you'll make a fine mother," she'd added with a smile.

But again Josef had spoiled things for her — for all of them. If only he had never gone

283

to Ontario. She sat on the porch swing, pushing it into motion with her bare foot, and wondered why she wasn't more upset with Luke. After all, Josef was simply delivering the news. Of course it was news that he had set out to discover, but there could be little question that there was at least some truth to the tale he had brought back with him from his travels north.

Still, Luke had kept things from her. How often had she asked him about his life before he came to Celery Fields? Now she remembered how early on when they first began keeping company he had avoided her questions and she had allowed it. He had always turned the subject back to her and she had allowed that, as well. Yet she could not deny that of late when he had tried to tell her about his past — about the events that had led up to his coming to Celery Fields — she had begged him not to speak of such things. "You are so very shallow, Greta Goodloe," she muttered angrily as she pushed the swing even harder.

"Careful there." Luke's voice came out of the dark and it took a moment for her to realize that he was standing in the shadow of the large oak tree next to the porch. "Wouldn't want you to go flying off that swing." His voice held none of the teasing she might have expected from such a comment. Indeed, he sounded sad and defeated. She longed to put her arms around him and tell him everything was going to work out for them. But she didn't know that. In fact it seemed more likely that things would not work out at all for them.

"Come and sit with me," she invited, fighting to keep her voice light when what she really wanted to do was cry out to him for answers. What would they do now? Why had he kept these things from her? Why hadn't he insisted that she listen? What had really happened back in his hometown?

"I shouldn't. If somebody saw us . . ."

"I don't care about that," she fumed, unable to hide her bad mood a second longer. She was so very tired of worrying about what other people might think. She needed to understand what *she* thought. That very morning she had thought that she was in love with this man, that they would be married and that by this time next year they might have that first baby. And like the sand castles the tourists' children built on the beach, all those plans and dreams had been swept away. Now what?

The silence that stretched between them at first made her think that Luke had perhaps gone home. But then she heard his step on the crushed calcified shells that lined the path leading up to the porch. She practically leaped from the swing and flung herself into his arms, burying her face against his chest, needing to hear the strong beat of his heart against her cheek. "Tell me that Josef made the whole thing up," she begged.

He wrapped his arms around her and rested his face against her hair. "You know better. Josef is an honorable man and even though he acted out of his deep caring for you, he would not lie to win favor with you."

It felt as if her heart had paused in its beating. She felt as if she could not find her next breath. "It's true then that you were placed under the *Bann*?"

"*Yah.* I was. I am."

"Then I will join you in that," she said firmly. Never had she been more certain of anything in her life.

Luke held her by her shoulders and moved her away from him so that she was looking up at him. "You will do no such thing," he said, his voice almost a growl. And he pulled her back against him. "I love you too much to let you throw your life away, Greta."

"Don't you understand that without you I have no life?"

"You don't know what you're saying."

She shoved away from him and returned to the swing, folding her arms across the bib of her apron as she glared at him. "Luke. I know exactly what I'm saying."

He did not move but remained standing on the top step of the porch. "No, I don't think you've thought this through. You'd lose everything — and you have a great deal to lose. Lydia — your family, this community that has been home for all of your life . . . if you had to leave all of that, never to see them or speak with them again?"

"I don't care," she muttered, but of course, she did care. Never to be able to see or speak with Lydia ever again? And what about Pleasant and her children — the children from her first marriage that Greta had come to love as if they were her very own? The twins from Pleasant's marriage to Jeremiah that Greta had rocked and made crib quilts for?

"You do care," Luke said. "You know that you do."

"But what about us?" She was very close to tears now. Then suddenly it hit her. "You're going away again, aren't you?" In the beat of hesitation he took before he sat down next to her on the swing, she had her answer. "No!" she cried.

Once again he wrapped her in his arms

and held her close. "Let's not get ahead of ourselves, Greta. There is one possibility that things might work out for us. If I agree to go back and seek forgiveness from the congregation in Ontario, then if the bishop there agrees to lift the *Bann,* I could come back and . . ."

"But you didn't do anything wrong," Greta protested. "Even Josef said that there were many who believed that . . ."

"What exactly did Josef tell you?"

"He told me the gist of it and after I left to find you, he told Lydia more of the details. There was a man who lived in your town and he had two daughters. As you told me, you had thought to court the younger one but the father wanted to be sure his elder daughter found a good husband." She paused and looked up at him, trying to read his expression in the dim light. "Josef told Lydia that the father offered you a large piece of land, a house and a great deal of money if you would marry the elder daughter."

"He did and I refused."

"Then he said the woman killed herself by jumping into the river, knowing it was far too cold to survive and also knowing that she could not swim."

"Josef has spoken the facts, Greta — at

least those that he knows. That is more or less what happened. The father — the deacon in the congregation — accused me of causing her death by breaking her heart, but there is one more part to the story — a part that the deacon never tells."

"Tell me."

"Her name was Dorie — the woman who drowned that day. She had heard her father make his offer to me. It was his offer that broke her heart."

"How can you know that?"

"Because she told me so. She came to my shop later that same day — it was just about dusk. She told me what she had overheard and she said that she was no more interested in a union with me than I was with her. She would not be bartered like one of her father's cows was the way she put it." His voice cracked on this last statement and Greta cupped his face with her hands. "Let me finish," he said.

"Yes, tell me everything and then maybe . . ."

"I offered to come with her so that we could both talk to her father, but she refused, saying that she wanted to take a walk along the river — as she often did — because she needed to think. Did she jump or slip? It had rained for days and the river bank would have been sodden and the puddles would have turned to black ice as the sun set. I have gone over it all a thousand times and I have no answer. If only I had insisted on seeing her home. I offered but she actually laughed and said that she thought the two of us had caused enough gossip for one lifetime. That's the way she said it — for one lifetime."

"What about the younger sister — the one you were in love with?"

He tightened his embrace. "I have already told you that I was never in love with her, Greta. You are the only woman I have ever loved. I need for you to believe that whatever may happen."

"But you had thought to marry her . . ."

"My brothers had all taken wives. *Dat* wanted to see us all settled. I thought perhaps she was a good choice. Our families had been neighbors."

"Did she love you?"

"I doubt it. I was several years older than she was. Rumor had it that she had set her sights on the bishop's youngest son."

"What happened after her sister died?"

"Nothing really. Her father forbade her having anything to do with me. I think she was relieved in one way and of course in time she came to believe what many others in town believed — that Dorie had jumped to her death because I rejected her."

"I'm sorry for Dorie," Greta said softly.

"You would have liked her. The truth of the matter is that if her father hadn't interfered, in time I probably would have chosen her on my own. We were a good match in age and temperament. But then I would never have come here — never met you — never known what true happiness can be."

He kissed her and it was not like the kisses they had shared before. This kiss held the taste of finality and she clung to him even as he gently pulled away.

"Just always remember that I love you, Greta Goodloe," he whispered and then he was gone, trudging down the lane to his shop without once looking back at her.

Everything in Greta's heart told her to run after him. Everything in her head told her that to do so would only make matters worse.

CHAPTER FOURTEEN

In the days between his Monday meeting with Levi and Bishop Troyer and Sunday, Luke first decided that he would spend his time working on the interior of his living quarters at the livery. But Roger Hadwell and others kept stopping by, offering to help or bringing a hot meal their wives had made for him and he did not like knowing that, if they knew what was coming on Sunday, they would not be offering such neighborly kindness. Besides, every time he looked out his window or stood at his door, he found himself looking straight at the Goodloe house.

So after a day of this, he spent the rest of the week calling on his customers in town, driving his wagon from farm to farm or house to house, offering to shoe a horse or repair some bit of hardware at no charge.

Finally the day he had dreaded arrived. On Sunday he did not attend the services

— held this time at Josef's farm. Early on Sunday morning he saw Lydia hitch up the buggy that she and Greta sometimes used for visiting or shopping. She led the horse around to the side of their house and after some time Luke saw Greta come out and join her sister for the ride to services. By the time they came back, he knew that everyone would know why, for the first time in weeks, the Goodloe sisters had arrived for services alone and Luke had not come at all.

At first Luke had thought the shunning would not bother him one way or another. After all he had been shunned before. And yet there was something at once familiar and at the same time strange about being shunned by his friends and neighbors in Celery Fields. In Ontario his father and brothers and their families had all taken part in shunning him — as was right within the guidelines of their faith. At family events he sat separate from everyone else to take his meals. Even when it was just his father and him sitting down for supper, Luke sat at a separate table and the two men did not exchange so much as a single word.

He had thought that being shunned in Celery Fields might be easier in some ways.

After all he already took his meals alone — separate from others. And he still had his *Englischer* customers who continued to patronize him, oblivious to the ways of the Amish. Business was slow and his days were long and silent. He had time on his hands that he spent completing the work on his upstairs rooms, sure now that he would need to make his home there instead of with Greta in the Obermeier house. He did not allow himself to think about how he was going to get through the days and weeks and years ahead without her.

One day he drove his wagon into Sarasota, intent on shopping for essentials such as pots and dishes that had not survived the fire. He ignored the curious stares of other shoppers as he drove down Main Street, navigating his team around the motorized vehicles that crowded the street. He found a place large enough to leave his wagon and team and climbed down to walk the half block to the hardware store. He knew and trusted the owner there. The man had sent him a good deal of business and had shown up to help with the rebuilding of his shop and livery. And while he would prefer doing business with Roger Hadwell or even the Yoders, he no longer had that choice.

Determined to make quick work of his errand, Luke reached for the doorknob even as he fumbled in his pocket for the shopping list he'd made that morning. The door flew open and he found himself looking straight into the eyes of Lydia Goodloe. For one long moment they stood there staring at each other. Lydia's mouth worked nervously as if she were fighting to hold back words, then she hurried past him without a word.

He stood in the doorway, watching her as she dodged other shoppers on her way to the bicycle that Luke had often seen Greta take to the beach. She dropped her shopping satchel into the large front basket before peddling toward him and on past the hardware without so much as a glance in his direction.

"Must be my day for the Amish," Jacob Olsen boomed from inside the store. "What can I do for you, Luke?"

Luke handed the proprietor his list, determined to make his purchases and leave as soon as possible. But his curiosity got the better of him as he waited for Jacob to gather the goods, then wrap and box them. "Does Lydia Goodloe come here to shop then?"

Jacob chuckled. "Only when Roger Hadwell runs out of stuff like the wallpaper paste she likes using for school projects."

"Wallpaper paste," Luke muttered.

"Yep, she can get pretty annoyed with Roger when he forgets to stock up although, if you ask me, she enjoys the excuse to come into town here now and again. For certain that pretty little sister of hers will find any reason to come here or head down to the bay." He chuckled and then licked the stub of a pencil as he figured the total. "You and Miss Goodloe have a spat, did you?"

Luke's expression must have mirrored the shock he felt at the unexpected question for Jacob hastened to add, "Thought I heard some time back that you and the school-teacher were . . ."

"Neh," Luke said as he handed over payment for the goods.

"My mistake." The clang of the cash register's bell was doubled by the jangle of the bells mounted above the front door. Both men glanced up to see the new customer. Both men's eyes widened in surprise when they saw Lydia standing in the doorway.

"Did you forget something, Miss Goodloe?" Jacob asked, coming from around the counter and walking up the long aisle to where she stood.

Luke felt rooted to the spot, his hand on

the box of goods he'd just purchased, his eyes darting around the store for some other exit that would save Lydia from having to openly shun him twice in one day.

"I . . . That is . . . I wondered if perhaps you might have something to recommend for cleaning seashells, Mr. Olsen? My sister is an avid collector and since I'm in town already, I thought perhaps you might know of something that makes the job easier. I know there are many of the tourists who collect when they are in town and . . ."

In all the time he'd known Lydia Goodloe, Luke did not think he had ever heard her string so many words together without so much as pausing for a breath.

"As a matter of fact," she continued, focusing all of her attention on Jacob, "my sister is at the bay right now and I thought that perhaps when she got home later I could surprise her." Luke found the way she had raised her voice and the emphasis she was placing on specific words mystifying. *At the bay right now.*

Surprise her.

Jacob held up a small brush. "This stiff bristle brush can do a good job of removing the barnacles and such without damaging the luster of the shell itself." He scurried down another aisle and returned with some small instruments. "These nut picks are good for the tighter places."

"I can see how they would do the job," Lydia said as she appeared to study the small tools Jacob held. "I'll take both the brush and the picks," she announced as she moved toward the counter, her eyes still avoiding any contact with Luke. She moved past him as if he weren't even there. "As I mentioned, Greta is even now at the bay. She's taken to spending several hours there in the afternoons and early evenings. The sunsets are something she especially enjoys."

"She stays there 'til dusk? How does she get back to Celery Fields?" Jacob had wrapped the brush and tools and made the necessary change while continuing the conversation.

For the first time since she'd returned to the store, Lydia's gaze flicked toward Luke, but then she turned her attention back to collecting her packages. "She usually has the bicycle but I needed it today so she walked. I do worry about her especially since those Amish who go there to fish always leave well before sunset. That and the fact that there are so many motorized vehicles on the road, but she insisted on going."

"She'll be all right," Jacob assured her. "I

hope these work out for her and if not, you tell her to stop by and we can see what else might be available."

"I appreciate that, Mr. Olsen. Good day to you."

Lydia turned and seemed once again about to sweep past Luke as if he were no more than one of the brooms and mops that Jacob had stacked in a barrel near the counter. But in the instant when they were side by side, she ducked her head as if to avoid any eye contact with him and he distinctly heard her whisper, "Go to her. She needs you."

Surely he had been mistaken. The very idea that Lydia Goodloe of all people might go against the *Ordnung* and actually speak to him was unthinkable. And yet after the evenings he'd spent with Greta, he understood the deep bond the two sisters shared. It was not out of the question that either sister would risk everything if faced with the choice of protecting or comforting the other. Lydia had given him a direct order. *Go to her.* Further she had provided him with Greta's whereabouts and the assurance that it would be safe for him to go there.

She needs you.

All that week Greta had made it her habit

to complete her chores as quickly as possible and then bicycle to the bay — the one place where she felt she could think. The bay was the one place where she did not have to see Luke moving in and out of his shop, dealing with the few customers who still came to him from Sarasota. The one place where she did not have to deliberately stay on the other side of the street to avoid the possibility of passing by him.

The bay had long been her refuge. Her father had brought her there often, once he realized that she enjoyed coming along whenever he went fishing there. He would wade out into the deeper water while she roamed the sandbar and shallow water closer to shore. After his death a year earlier she had started coming alone. Odd, she thought now, that not once had she ever thought of asking Josef to come with her. Odd, that all she could think about lately was sharing the spot with Luke.

As the announcement of their plans to wed drew closer, she had thought about all the times they would share here. He would learn to fish — and perhaps teach their sons to fish, as well. She and the girls would look for shells and she would teach them to respect the precious life forms that inhabited the conchs and whelks and other species making their home in the calm, warm waters of the bay.

She stubbed her toe and gave a little cry of surprise mingled with pain. She'd left her shoes on the grass near the narrow sand strip where it was easiest to enter the water. She knew better than not to pay attention to where she was walking. Many of the shells had razor sharp edges and others were round and smooth and slippery enough to cause her to lose her balance. She hopped on one foot for a few seconds until the initial shot of pain waned, then bent to find the culprit.

Buried deep in the muck with only its spiraled end partially exposed was a lightening whelk that, given the width of its exposed end, was possibly the largest specimen she had ever seen. Gently she tugged at it and knew it still held its tenant when it resisted her pull. She bent down, uncaring that the hem of her skirt was getting soaked, and pushed away the wet sand until the length of it was exposed. It had to be nearly twelve inches in length. With great care she urged it to release its hold and when it came free with a sucking sound that made her smile, she needed both hands to support the weight of it. With care and wonder she turned it over in time to see the slick black foot of the sea animal slide back inside the shelter of the shell and close the hard aperture or door that kept out intruders like her.

The outside rim of the shell was a pearly opalescent white that caught the late afternoon sun and turned it into rainbows of color. Greta ran her thumb over the shell, marveling at how the exposed part that she had stubbed her toe on was rough and barnacle covered, while this underside was so beautiful that it brought tears to her eyes. Reluctantly she turned the whelk over again and set it precisely into the indented spot it had occupied before she'd disturbed it.

"Sorry," she whispered, "but thank you for being there and for reminding me that even when something appears so worn and scarred on the one side, it might just be protecting something perfect and precious underneath." She stayed there for several long minutes, watching over the whelk as it settled itself more firmly into the sand. It would not be there tomorrow or even an hour from now, she knew.

Many times she had followed the trails of various species left behind like footprints in the sand, hoping to come upon the creature itself. But usually the trail eventually disappeared — not unlike the footprints she was leaving as she moved on across the damp sandbar toward the beds of clamshells that marked the place where an inland bayou emptied into the bay. Not unlike the joys of her life had disappeared, she thought now, unable to stem the roil of bitterness and disappointment that rose in her throat like nausea.

"I know that it is not my place to question You, Heavenly Father," she said aloud as she walked. "But I am so very confused. What is it that You want of me? And Luke? He is a good man — kind and caring of others. Please take this burden from him — from us both."

But she knew that such a thing was unlikely. Lydia had learned from Hannah Harnischer, whose husband Levi was the church deacon, that to go against the ruling of another congregation — even one in Canada — was simply not done. "Of course, there is always the possibility that Bishop Troyer will consider the fact that Luke has already suffered mightily in all of this," Lydia had hastened to add, no doubt aware of the pain that her news was causing Greta.

"It hardly matters, Liddy," Greta had told her. "Even if the bishop recommends leniency, the congregation still must vote unanimously to accept his ruling and we both know that Josef will never vote in favor of such a thing."

The way that Liddy had looked down before forcing a half smile and murmuring something about trusting in God had told Greta that she was right. And so her task when she came to the bay was to pray for guidance. What plan did God have in mind for her? And because she had never believed that God was either cruel or vengeful she knew that indeed there had to be some purpose in all that had happened.

She stared out toward the horizon where the sun was beginning to tinge the clouds with pinks and lavenders. Soon it would be dusk. She should start for home. Liddy would worry, especially since Greta did not have their bicycle for transportation. The walk home would take some time and if she didn't start right away it would be well after dark when Greta arrived.

But still she lingered, searching for answers that refused to come and grieving for all that she and Luke might have shared.

Luke was in such a rush to follow Lydia's instructions that he almost forgot to take the box of goods that Jacob had packed for him. And he did not miss the odd look followed by the sly grin as Jacob called him back to remind him.

"I expect you can still catch up to her," Jacob said with a chuckle and a nod toward the street where Lydia Goodloe was peddling past on her bicycle.

Luke set the box of pans and dishes into the back of his wagon, taking care to pad the box with some old horse blankets to keep them from sliding around. Instead of turning the wagon north toward Celery Fields at the end of Main Street, he turned south and followed the road as it curved along the bay, his eyes peeled for any sign of Greta. He passed fishermen on their way home for the day as well as women from town pushing baby prams. Several drivers honked their car horns at him as they impatiently sped past him, causing his team to shy and stumble.

Realizing that he'd be better off on foot, Luke found a place to leave his wagon and team and retraced his steps along the calm waters of Sarasota Bay. He had nearly given up when he spotted a movement near the bend where the street curved east and there she was, not twenty yards from where he stood. Her head was bowed as she studied the clear water that covered her ankles and feet and soaked the hem of her dress. Her bonnet obscured her face but he would

305

know her form and movements anywhere.

He took a moment to pull off his shoes and socks and set them next to hers on the narrow patch of sand that could not be called a beach. Then he waded into the water, surprised at its warmth and at the soft sandy muck that instantly covered his feet. He uttered a grunt as he pulled his feet free and Greta looked around.

"You do not need to say anything or even look at me," he said as he worked his way closer to her much as he might have approached a skittish horse. But instead of shying away she splashed her way through the shallow water until she was standing within a breath of him. He had to clench his fists to keep from pulling her into his arms.

He needn't have bothered trying to restrain himself for after only an instant she flung herself against him, her arms wrapped around his waist as she pressed her cheek to his chest. "Oh, Luke, what are we going to do?"

Instinctively he completed the circle of their embrace and rested his cheek against the top of her bonnet. "We will do whatever God wills," he told her.

She looked up at him and her expression

was one of such fury that he was taken aback.

"And what if God wills it that . . ." She seemed incapable of finishing her thought.

"Then His will be done," Luke said. "You know that's the way of it. It is not for us to decide or to know what the future holds, Greta."

"But I love you," she fumed.

"Enough to let me go?"

Now she stepped away from him. "You are leaving?"

"I may have to, Greta. I cannot sustain a business in a community where I am shunned."

"You could find another way to make our living — farming. If we farmed then we could live away from town and . . ."

Luke pulled her to him again, aware of the last rays of sun streaking the sky behind her. "Sh-h-h," he coaxed. "Think how hard it would be for you to live so near to Lydia and the rest of your family and yet never be able to visit or share in their joys. Think how lonely life would become for you. In time you would rightly come to resent making such a choice."

"Never."

"Do not say that, Greta. It is because you cannot know the toll such a decision might take that you must trust in God to lead you in the right way. At this moment I know it seems like everything is going wrong but you have to trust me. I have traveled this road before. It led me to you at a time when I thought that my life was doomed."

"And then why would God bring us both such happiness only to snatch it away again?"

Her logic was simplistic and yet he had no answer for her, nothing he could say that would ease her pain and stress. The truth was that in the still darkness of the night he had asked himself — and God — that very same question. And maybe in that doubt lay the answer. "Greta, I do not have the solution to this struggle we face but I have faith that God does. If we are patient in time . . ."

"We don't have time," she argued. "The vote is to be taken on Sunday and even if Bishop Troyer recommends forgiveness and leniency . . ."

Luke pressed his finger to her lips. "Walk with me," he invited as he took her hand and stepped onto a sandbar that had formed close to the shoreline. "Let's enjoy the sunset together."

Together they followed the line of the sandbar until they were standing several feet from the shore, water surrounding them, the sounds of the town settling in for the evening behind them. Luke stared at the lines of vermilion and orange that stretched out across the horizon as the fiery ball of the sun appeared to sink into the water. He put his arm around Greta's shoulder and drew her closer. "There was a time when I stood on the banks of a rushing river, Greta, knowing that Dorie had died there. The day was waning and it had been a day of storms and darkness. But as I stood there I looked up and on the horizon I saw a single ray of light breaking through the layers of thunderclouds. I clung to that ray of light then, Greta, as you must cling to this beautiful sunset today."

He looked down at her and saw that she was frowning.

"Promise me, Greta," he urged. "Promise me that whatever happens you will not lose faith."

"I promise — I will not lose faith. But I also will not lose hope."

He framed her earnest face with his palms and kissed her, knowing that this might be his last chance. Her response to his lips meeting hers was almost more than he could bear, but after a long moment he tore himself away. "We have to go."

"I know," Greta sighed. "I am later than usual and Lydia will be worried."

"Your sister knows you are with me," Luke admitted. "She sent me to find you."

Greta shook her head and smiled her first smile since he had found her. "She is always watching out for me."

"And that is why I know that whatever happens, you will be all right." He laced his fingers in hers and led the way back to where they had left their shoes. Greta stooped to wipe his feet dry with the skirt of her apron. When he reached for his socks, she took them from him and tugged first one and then the other onto his feet, then did the same with his shoes.

All the while the looks they exchanged said plainly that they were performing the sacred ritual of the washing of the feet. In services men washed the feet of other men and women washed the feet of other women, but it felt absolutely right and proper that Luke and Greta should be performing this ritual together. When she had finished, she sat on the grass while he rubbed her feet dry and brushed away the last remnants of sand with his hands, then seeing that she had worn no stockings, he placed first one shoe and then the other on her feet.

And in the tradition of their faith, once the ritual was completed they clasped hands and kissed each other lightly.

"Da Herr sei mit uns," Luke murmured.

"The Lord be with us," Greta repeated then added, "Amen, in Peace."

"Amen, zum vreda," Luke repeated as he silently prayed that it would be so.

CHAPTER FIFTEEN

There was hardly a place left to park their buggy when Greta and Lydia arrived at Levi Harnischer's farm for services. The crowded yard was certainly no surprise. Everyone knew that on this day Luke's future in Celery Fields would be decided. For two long weeks Greta's thoughts had seesawed between wishing this day would come and dreading that it ever would. For today Bishop Troyer would make his recommendation to the congregation regarding Luke's fate. Then the congregation would vote as to whether or not they would accept that recommendation. The vote had to be unanimous and therein lay the problem.

If Bishop Troyer should recommend leniency, Greta knew that there was no possible way that Josef would vote in favor of forgiving Luke and accepting him back into the Celery Fields congregation. For the hundredth time she considered the idea of standing with Luke either way, thus assuring that if the vote went against him then she, too, would be shunned and placed under the *Bann.* But they could go somewhere new — start over . . .

As if reading her thoughts, Lydia leaned close. "Do not act rashly, sister," she said softly. "Whatever the day brings you must accept that this is God's will and He alone can determine the course your life must take going forward."

"I am not thinking of myself," Greta grumbled. "I am thinking of Luke."

Lydia lifted one skeptical eyebrow, then led the way inside the farmhouse where a hush fell over the women gathered in the front hall. By now everyone knew that it was Greta that Luke had courted all these weeks. It was Greta who would be heartbroken — again. Like clusters of sea grass along the shore, they parted to allow the two sisters to pass on their way to the kitchen — where yet another silence surrounded them. They set the baskets of food they'd brought for the meal after services and then without a word Lydia led the way into the front room where they took their places on the bench reserved for the unmarried females.

They had arrived late — Greta's fault. She

had dawdled longer than usual over dressing that morning and then she had burned their breakfast and insisted on making a second round of food. Lydia had not protested and Greta was grateful that her sister seemed to understand her need to avoid arriving for services a minute sooner than absolutely necessary.

Slowly and silently the room filled. There were so many people present that it became necessary to press closer together on the narrow benches and Greta found herself pinned between Lydia on one side and Esther Yoder on the other. Across the aisle and at the far end of a row sat Josef. He was positioned closest to the door. If only she could come up with some way to get him out the door before Bishop Troyer announced his recommendation and the vote was called. She squeezed her eyes shut to stem the wave of rage she felt toward Josef. He had ruined her future with his meddling and for what? Hadn't he been the one to quit her?

She felt Lydia's nudge and opened her eyes as the congregation stood for the singing of the first hymn. The service had begun. In just three hours, it would be over and then . . .

Her heart hammered and her knees

seemed to hold no strength for standing. She wavered and Lydia glanced her way — as did Esther. "Are you all right, Greta?" Esther asked in a tone that oozed concern but came from a mouth that was fighting a smirk.

"I am fine." Greta straightened, locking her knees to maintain her posture. She had less than three hours now to come up with some plan, some way to save Luke, for she knew that he would never allow her to stand with him if the decision went against him. She heard nothing of the sermons delivered first by the second minister and then by Bishop Troyer. Three hours passed and she was still no closer to coming up with a plausible strategy. She made her lips move during the singing of the final hymn but no sound came out as she gripped her side of the *Ausband* that she was sharing with Lydia. Instead she silently repeated the same phrase again and again — *Help me please!*

Finally the service ended and Bishop Troyer stepped to the front of the room. He stood for a moment as quiet settled over the congregation. Everyone knew what was coming and the tension in the crowded room was palpable. Bishop Troyer cleared his throat, then bowed his head in silent prayer. Everyone else in the room followed suit. After what seemed an eternity, he cleared his throat again and there was a general rustling of bodies as everyone turned their attention to him.

"We have before us today a most serious business," he began. "Luke Starns came to us nearly a year ago. He bought a business and has served his customers fairly and well these last months. He has attended services without fail and made himself available to serve others in need. He has in short made every effort to be a good neighbor and friend to everyone living here in Celery Fields — as we have been to him in return, for he has been as a brother."

Greta saw a few men nod involuntarily and took hope from the action. But Josef's scowl only deepened as he leaned forward as if to stop the bishop's praise of Luke.

"The charges against Luke Starns in his former community are not to be taken lightly," Bishop Troyer continued. "I have spoken with him at length about this matter and he has requested the opportunity to come before you today to have his say before I offer you my recommendation for his future with this congregation."

There was a gasp of surprise and Josef was practically halfway out of his seat when

Luke entered the room from the small bedroom where he'd obviously been waiting. He looked worn and exhausted, the lines around his eyes and mouth more pronounced than Greta recalled. He stood before the bishop for a moment and then turned to face the congregation. He glanced around and for a brief moment his gaze settled on her. She gave him what she hoped was an expression that mirrored her firm belief in him and her determination to stand with him no matter what.

The flicker of a smile skated across his lips but it was gone before it could blossom as he focused his attention on the rest of the congregation. He straightened to his full height and allowed his eyes to skim over every member of the congregation before speaking. Everyone leaned forward to catch every word.

"You have all by now heard some version of my situation in Ontario," he began, his voice raspy as if he badly needed a drink of water. Bishop Troyer moved a step closer to him, but Luke just kept talking. "I have explained to the bishop and deacon and other leaders of this congregation what happened there and why in the end I acted as I did. I am deeply grateful for their willingness to hear me and for the way you —" He raised his hand and gestured toward those seated before him. "The way you have held me in your thoughts and prayers during these difficult days. I want you to know that whatever comes of this, the community of Celery Fields will always be a place that I think of as my home. I have come here today to seek your forgiveness. I have wronged you — especially some of you . . ." His eyes darted toward Greta then back to the others. "I ask your forgiveness for not revealing the circumstances that brought me to Celery Fields. I ask your forgiveness for placing this entire community in a difficult position as it relates to the *Ordnung* and this congregation's relationship with the greater church. I ask your forgiveness for my arrogance in thinking that I could manage the business of my past alone. And I assure you that whatever the outcome may be, I accept that as my doing and no one else's. God's will be done."

He sat down then, his shoulders hunched tensely, his hands clenched together. Greta had never wanted to go to him more than she did in that moment. She wanted to wrap her arms around those broad shoulders and assure him that everything would work out. God would see to it. But as a low murmur made its way across the room, Bishop

Troyer raised his hands and said, "I am prepared to offer my recommendation for the vote of this congregation. Before I do, let us all bow our heads once more in silent prayer as we seek God's guidance in this matter."

Greta bowed her head but she kept her eyes riveted on Josef. He sat upright, his eyes focused coldly on Luke, his arms folded across his chest in a gesture so completely devoid of forgiveness that Greta felt physically ill. Bile rose in her throat as beads of sweat lined her upper lip and forehead.

She stood up and let out a low moan as she clutched her stomach. "I need some air," she whispered as she clamored over Esther Yoder and headed for the door. She was aware that Lydia had followed her as she ran from the house and out onto the porch. But far more important was the fact that Josef had followed her, as well. As she clung to a post that supported the covering over the porch, he came to her.

"Greta?"

"I'll be all right," she assured him. "It was just so very close in there and . . ."

Josef took hold of her elbow and led her to a chair. Lydia came running from the kitchen with a glass of water.

"This has been too much for her," Lydia said, her words directed at Josef. "What is your purpose in all of this, Josef Bontrager?"

"I care for your sister," Josef snapped defiantly. "A great deal."

"You have an odd way of showing that care," Lydia groused as she used a handkerchief to wipe the perspiration from Greta's brow.

"No more arguing," Greta said softly as she heard the low murmur of Bishop Troyer's voice and knew the vote was imminent. And in that moment she knew that she must allow whatever was about to happen without her interfering. She had no doubt that Josef would stay with her even if that meant that he would miss the vote. And if the bishop recommended leniency, as he seemed inclined to do given the way he had allowed Luke to address the congregation, then Josef's absence gave Luke the best possible chance to have things turn out in his favor and therefore to turn out well for them. But she found that she could not tamper with whatever course God had set for Luke. She would place her faith in His will.

"They are about to take the vote, Josef. You should go back inside," she said softly. "I will be fine and Lydia is here. Go on."

Josef straightened and looked at her for a long moment. She met his gaze and knew that he understood what she was doing. "Luke's fate — and mine — are in your hands, Josef," she said softly. "Isn't that what you wanted?"

"No," he protested. "I only wanted to be sure you would be happy — that you would not cast your lot with a man who . . ."

"Makes me happier than I have ever dreamed possible?"

Josef looked out toward the horizon where the sky had darkened and a thunderstorm threatened. "I wanted to be that person," he admitted. Then he looked back at her. "But I never was, was I? I mean we were good friends — the best of friends but . . ."

"We are and ever shall be the very best of friends, Josef. Now please go," Greta urged. *Before I change my mind and do whatever it takes to keep you here.* She turned away as she felt the tears she'd held in check all morning start to spill. She buried her face in Lydia's apron as her sister wrapped her arms around her, crooning to her that all would be well. And when she looked up to protest that idea, she saw that Josef had gone back inside and through the open window she heard Bishop Troyer clear his throat and then call for the vote.

She clutched Lydia's apron in her fists as the tears leaked down her cheeks and onto her dress. From inside she heard a chorus of Ayes.

"And those against the recommendation for forgiveness and reinstatement?" the bishop said.

Greta held her breath.

There was no sound except the rumble of distant thunder.

"Then we are agreed," Bishop Troyer said softly.

And then even as there was an outpouring of relief and warm greetings for Luke inside the house, the skies opened up and released a downpour. The storm that had seemed so ominous just minutes earlier now seemed to release all of the fear and tension that Greta had been holding in check these last weeks. It was over. Truly over.

She looked up at Lydia who was beaming at her. "Feeling a little better, are we?" she teased.

Greta laughed and then she saw Luke standing in the doorway and uncaring of protocol or rules, she ran to him, stopping just short of embracing him. Instead she touched his cheek. "It is at an end?" she asked, her voice seeking his assurance.

"Neh," he said, "For us it is just the begin-

ning." And then he grinned at her and before she could say anything more the two of them were swept back inside the house in a circle of friends and family as everyone hurried to set out the meal they would all share.

CHAPTER SIXTEEN

Greta awoke on her wedding day to find Lydia preparing their breakfast. Set on the table by Greta's plate was a small covered jar. "Oh, Liddy, it's some of Pleasant's starter for sourdough, isn't it?"

Lydia smiled. "Pleasant brought it by yesterday."

The tradition of a mother giving her daughter a jar of the base for making the traditional bread the way she'd been given a jar on her wedding day was an old one. Greta had often thought about her mother as she baked bread for herself and Lydia through the years. But their mother had been so young when she died and in truth their older half sister had been their only true mother for all of their childhood.

"Pleasant and I set it to ripen at the bakery so you wouldn't accidentally see it at her house."

Greta hugged Lydia tight. "It's the very

best wedding present, Liddy. Thank you."

Lydia pulled back and studied Greta closely. "Are you ready, Greta?"

Mistaking her sister's concern as that of asking about the preparations, Greta laughed. "I think so. I'm glad we decided on setting up the food in the barn. The house is bound to be stifling by noon and . . ."

"I'm asking if you are sure, Greta," Lydia said softly as she touched Greta's cheek. "Is Luke Starns the man you wish to spend the rest of your days with?"

"Oh, yes," Greta said without hesitation. "I love him so very much that sometimes my heart hurts from the fullness of that love."

Lydia smiled. "Then let's get you married."

Together the sisters walked through the small farmhouse that they had shared their whole lives. Some of the larger pieces of furniture had been moved down to Luke's shop to make room for the benches and extra seating that would accommodate the guests for the ceremony. There was little doubt that every Amish family that lived within ten miles of Celery Fields would be there along with many families from further north — as far away as Ontario — that would travel south to celebrate the occasion. In the kitchen they could hardly find space to set a single dish, so filled were the counters with the variety of cakes that Pleasant had created for the occasion.

Towering above the others was the wedding cake — a four-layer confection with each layer being nearly six inches thick. Pleasant had piled on white frosting, covered the confection with shredded coconut and studded the entire cake with tiny silver candies. To either side of the main cake was a smaller cake frosted and decorated with the words "Best Wishes" on one and "Good Luck" on the other. These three cakes would make up what was known as the "wedding corner" — the place where Greta and Luke and the members of their wedding party would sit for the meal following the ceremony.

"Did Luke bring the dishes?" Greta asked. Tradition held that the groom provided the dishes for the wedding party's meal as a gift to his bride.

"He did, but he made me promise not to set them out until after the ceremony."

"Is he afraid I'll change my mind?" Greta asked. She had meant the comment to sound light and teasing but her voice caught.

"Not at all," Lydia reassured her. "He wants to surprise you is all."

"Well, I have a surprise for him, as well," Greta said.

"Hello," someone called out from the back porch.

"It's Pleasant and the others!" Greta cried and ran to greet the women who had arrived early to finish the preparations for the big day. "Now we can make the Nothings and finish decorating the tables."

Nothings, a traditional pastry for weddings, were nothing more than round concave saucer-sized pieces of dough, deep-fried and sprinkled with powdered sugar. They were stacked around the cakes in the wedding corner and on the larger table that held the cakes and pies for the guests. In addition to the piles of Nothings, each table for guests held a glass vase filled with stalks of celery. It was an old tradition, as well, but seemed especially applicable to their community of Celery Fields.

"Oh, it's going to be such a wonderful day," Greta squealed as she ran from house to barn and back again, checking to be sure everything was just exactly as she had always imagined it would be.

"You have been planning this wedding day from the time you were five," Pleasant said, laughing at her half sister as Greta traded one bunch of celery for another with more foliage. "Why wouldn't everything be perfect?"

Greta grinned. "There are always surprises," she reminded Pleasant.

"Yes, well, in your case I think we've had all the surprises we can take."

All of the women joined in the laughter that followed as they worked in happy concert to prepare everything for Greta's wedding day.

Because others had been steadily arriving all morning, the kitchen rang with laughter and excited chatter of the women. On the porch several young girls gathered in clusters, whispering and giggling together. In the yard the men and boys stood around sharing stories about the coming growing season or the price of crops while the younger children raced around, infected by the excitement of the day.

"You keep looking out that window as if you are expecting someone," Pleasant said.

"I had hoped . . ." Greta's voice trailed off and then a moment later she let out a whoop of excitement as she raced out to the porch and pointed to a wagon pulling up to Luke's shop.

■ ■ ■ ■

Luke had just finished dressing when he heard the creak of wagon wheels outside and realized that the vehicle was not following the lane that ran up to the Goodloe house as every other wagon or buggy had that morning. This one had instead stopped in front of his shop.

Figuring that it was one of his *Englischer* customers with some emergency, Luke sighed and headed down to his shop. After all, business was business and these days he could not afford to turn anyone away. He just hoped that he could persuade whoever it was to let him get married first before he fixed whatever was broken.

He walked through the livery part of his business to the blacksmith shop in front and pulled open one of the large double doors.

"Guten . . ."

The rest of his greeting lodged in his throat as he saw his father being helped down from the wagon by his three brothers. The four men of his family lined up and faced him. Behind them, still in the wagon, were his sisters-in-law and at least a dozen children and all of them seemed to be holding their breath.

"Son," his father said huskily and Luke stumbled forward to embrace the elderly man.

There was a moment of hushed respectful silence and then one of the children asked, "Are we going to stay?"

"Yah," Luke's father said before anyone else could answer. He touched Luke's cheek. "We are going to stay."

And then everyone was climbing down from the wagon and Luke was greeting his brothers and their wives and the nieces and nephews he had not seen in months and two new ones that he had not met at all.

"How did . . . Why . . ."

"We had a letter — two," his brother told him. "One from your bishop and another from Greta Goodloe."

"Greta wrote to you?"

"Yah," his youngest brother replied with a laugh. "She made a good case, brother — for you and for us moving down here where as she said 'it hardly ever snows.' "

Everyone laughed at that and Luke realized that they already liked Greta even before they'd had a chance to meet her. Then his father took hold of his arm.

"Your bishop wrote to our bishop, Luke. It has been decided that while you are still under the *Bann* back home, you have made your amends with the community here. Since you would not be able to come to us under those conditions, we decided to come here."

"To stay?"

"We'll see," his father said, glancing around and seeming to find the town to his liking. "After the wedding, we can decide."

"You are still planning to get married today, aren't you?" his eldest brother teased.

Luke looked up toward the Goodloe house and saw that Greta had come out onto the porch and was watching the reunion from that safe distance. The way she had knotted the skirt of her apron in one hand told him that she was worried things might not go as planned. "Come and meet Greta and her sister," Luke said and as he helped his father back onto the wagon and then led the team of horses up the lane, Greta came running to meet them.

By the time everyone had been introduced and Pleasant had insisted on feeding all of Luke's family, it was time for Greta to get dressed. Lydia and Pleasant would serve as her attendants and they followed her to her bedroom to help her get ready. Her dress — a deep green with a white apron and *kapp* — hung on a peg. Today she would exchange the black *kapp* she had worn all her life for the white prayer covering of a married woman. When she died — hopefully years hence — she would be buried in this same dress.

There was a lot of excited chatter as the women helped her bundle her thick hair into a smooth knot and held the dress while she pinned it into place with the series of black straight pins laid out on her bureau. Then came the apron and last of all the starched prayer *kapp*.

There was no mirror but when Greta turned she could see in the eyes of her sisters that she looked beautiful.

"Oh, Greta," Lydia whispered as tears welled up in her eyes. "You look like Mama." It was the most loving thing that Lydia could have said. Greta had little memory of their mother but Lydia had often told her stories about how beautiful their mother was, how kind and giving and admired she was.

"I only hope I can live up to her legacy," she told Lydia.

"You already have," Pleasant assured her. "Now, let's go get you married."

As she stepped out into the narrow hallway, Greta saw Luke standing in the front room with his brothers, talking quietly to

Bishop Troyer. He was dressed in a black suit and as tradition dictated, for the first and only time in his life he was wearing a tie. As if he had sensed her presence, he looked up and the smile that lit his face was the only sign she needed that he was as anxious as she was for their life together to begin.

Lydia placed a hand on Greta's waist and guided her toward the front row of benches where she sat with Luke and his brothers as well as Lydia and Pleasant. They were the bridal party and now that they were in place the guests would begin to take their seats in the rows of benches behind them. At the stroke of nine in the morning the singing began and Bishop Troyer and the other ministers for the day left the room with Greta and Luke following them.

In Lydia's bedroom, the couple sat next to each other on Lydia's bed while Bishop Troyer instructed them on the duties of marriage and all the while Greta could hear the singing from the front room. She thought she had never heard anything so beautiful in her life. Now as Luke took her hand and together they followed the ministers back into the front room, Greta felt a kind of serenity come over her. Usually she was restless and distracted during services, but not today. Throughout the three-hour service she sat as still as a stone, her fingers woven together with Luke's as the bishop told the stories of marriages from the Old Testament — from Adam and Eve to Isaac and Rebekah.

Finally Bishop Troyer called Luke and Greta to come forward. He smiled at them and without benefit of notes he began the marriage ceremony.

"You have heard the ordinance of Christian wedlock presented," he intoned. "Are you now willing to enter wedlock together as God has ordained and commanded?"

"Yes," Luke and Greta chorused.

He turned to Luke. "Are you confident that this, our sister, is ordained of God to be your wedded wife?"

Luke's response was immediate and rang out clearly in the silent room. "Yes."

Bishop Troyer turned to Greta. "Are you confident that this, our brother, is ordained of God to be your wedded husband?"

The memory of all that she and Luke had had to endure over these last months ran through Greta's mind like a rush of wind before a storm. But then she looked up at him and saw in his eyes the calm and peace of certainty. "Yes," she replied.

"Do you also promise your wedded wife,

before the Lord and his church, that you will nevermore depart from her, but will care for her and cherish her, if bodily sickness comes to her, or in any circumstances which a Christian husband is responsible to care for, until the dear God will again separate you from each other?"

"Yes."

He repeated the question to Greta and she had to physically restrain herself from cupping Luke's cheek as she replied, "I promise."

The bishop then placed his hand over Luke and Greta's joined hands and intoned, "So then I may say with Raguel, the God of Abraham, the God of Isaac and the God of Jacob be with you and help you together and fulfill His blessing abundantly upon you, through Jesus Christ. Amen."

And so they were married. There were no exclamations of congratulations as the couple made their way from the house to the barn where they took their place in the wedding corner. Luke sat to Greta's right and when all the guests had gathered, the bishop gave the signal for silent prayer. Beneath the table Luke held fast to Greta's hand as they bowed their heads. And then as if a signal had been given, every head lifted and the room exploded with conversation and laughter all interrupted by the occasional song. The festivities continued on through the afternoon and well into the evening. And through it all Greta was aware of only one person — Luke, her husband.

While tradition held that the couple spend their first night in the home of the bride's parents, Luke had asked Lydia if it would be all right with her for him to take Greta to the home he'd prepared for them instead.

"Of course," Lydia replied. "If *Maemm und Dat* were still alive, they would want to follow tradition, but in this case I think everyone will understand. Besides we need the extra space. Your father will stay here with your brother Ivan and his family while all the rest go to stay with Pleasant and Jeremiah. It's all arranged."

"Denki," Luke said, unable to disguise the relief he felt that Lydia — as usual — had taken charge of everything and left him and Greta with nothing to think about except starting their life together.

So when the last guest had gone home and all of the food and tables and chairs had been put away, he took Greta's arm and led her outside. "Come take a ride with me," he said.

She did not protest but looked up at him

the way she had looked at him throughout the long day — as if she were certain that he could do anything. She did giggle a little when he helped her into Jeremiah's open-topped buggy. "Why, Luke Starns, don't tell me that at long last you have bought yourself a proper courting buggy," she teased.

"I borrowed it from Jeremiah — or rather from Caleb. It's his buggy and I don't think he was very pleased with having to loan it to me tonight. I'm pretty sure he had his heart set on seeing Bettina home."

Greta snuggled close to him and sighed. "I expect there will be a wedding there within the next year," she said and yawned as she let her head rest on Luke's shoulder. But when he called for the horse to stop barely five minutes after they'd left Lydia's house, Greta sat up and looked around. "Why are we stopping here?" Greta asked sleepily when she realized that Luke had pulled up the buggy to the old Obermeier place. "I don't like this place."

"Truly?" Luke pretended to consider the large old ramshackle house that had sat forlorn and unoccupied at the far end of the main street ever since Pleasant and Jeremiah had married. "I was thinking it would make a good place for us to live — right here in town, close to my place of business and Lydia."

Greta shuddered, fighting an obvious case of nerves as he came around the buggy and helped her down.

"Let's just go have a look."

They walked up the front path together. "I suppose it could work," Greta said hesitantly. "Perhaps after we return from our trip I could invite the other women for a frolic to help me get it fixed up properly."

"I thought we might stay here tonight," Luke said, barely able to keep the smile he was trying to hide in check when she gasped audibly and turned to face him.

"Tonight? But . . ."

"Sure. It's pretty crowded at your sister's place and . . ."

"But, Luke, there are bound to be cob-webs and what about furniture — where would we sleep?"

"I thought perhaps we might sleep up there," he said, pointing to an upstairs window where a lamp glowed.

"Someone is here," she whispered. "The front door is open."

"*Yah.* Others have been here getting things ready," Luke explained.

He held open the screen door and waited for her to enter first. The scent of lemon oil rose from the wood-planked floors and the banister that led to the second floor. The place was spotless and completely furnished. They might have lived there already for years and just be coming home from a visit with friends, Greta thought.

"Oh, Luke, is it truly to be our home?"

Now he laughed out loud. "I thought you didn't like this place."

"I didn't but, oh, Luke, look at it." She clapped her hands together in delight and spun around, trying to take in everything at once. She grabbed his hand and pulled him down the hall. "I want to see the kitchen," she exclaimed.

Luke followed her willingly and stood quietly in the doorway as she examined the dishes — already washed after their use for the wedding and stored on the open shelves — and a few pots and pans polished to a high shine and hanging from hooks overhead. He was well aware that they would be adding to the collection as they visited Greta's extended family in the Midwest.

"It's everything I ever dreamed it would be," she murmured, running her hand lightly over the table that dominated the center of the large room. "We can fit half a dozen children around this table at least."

Luke chuckled and came to her, lifting her so that she was sitting on the counter near the window. "In the morning look out this window and you'll see the kitchen garden that Liddy planted for you."

She cupped his face in her hands. "You have made me so very happy," she said softly.

With great care and tenderness he removed her prayer covering and set it aside, and then he pulled out the pins that held her hair, freeing it to fall over her shoulders and down her back. Using his fingers he combed through the curls that sprang back to life after being confined for hours. "Your curls are like you," he teased, "oh so properly controlled when necessary but set free to have their own way, they scatter like the shorebirds taking flight."

"Now you listen to me," she said with mock sternness, "I have taken to heart my responsibilities now that we are married. Please don't worry that I will . . ."

He buried his face in the masses of her long hair that he held in his hands and shook his head. Then he raised his face to hers. "I love you as you are, Greta. I want your lightheartedness to fill these rooms like sunlight. I want to come home at the end of every day knowing that here waiting for me is my wife with her laughter that is like music and her smile that takes away all my

340

weariness and worries."

"And on those days when I may not be smiling or laughing?"

"Then I will come home and hold you and care for you until the lightness and the laughter return," he promised.

"I am sometimes given to tears," she warned, stroking her fingers through his thick hair.

He laughed. "I well remember that. After all, on our first real meeting it was your tears that stirred the embers of my attraction to you." But then he saw her face lit by the full moon and her beauty took his breath away. "You are my wife, Greta, and never has God blessed a man more."

Greta flung her arms around his neck. "You know what I wish? I wish this day would never end."

"It is only the first of many days, Greta. Days that we will fill with laughter and tears and memories and, if God grants it, the blessing of children."

"Oh, you want children, do you, Luke Starns?" she teased.

"Well, we do have that large table we need to fill." But he knew that he sounded less than absolutely certain about their future. "You do want children, don't you?"

"I do," she replied and as she placed her

lips on his, she added, "And if those chairs are to ever get filled, we'd best get started, don't you think?"

With a roar of laughter, Luke scooped her high in his arms and carried her up the stairs to the large bedroom that overlooked the main street of Celery Fields. And as she settled under the light cotton quilt with Luke for their first night as husband and wife, Greta gave thanks and also begged God's forgiveness for ever doubting that His intent all along had been to bring this stranger from Ontario to Florida — and into her life.

Dear Reader,

Well, bless everyone out there who asked for more brides from Celery Fields! I'm delighted to have the opportunity to tell the stories of Pleasant's half sisters, Greta and Lydia. This is Greta's story with Lydia's to follow. As I put this story together I found myself working from the premise that while God guides our path in this world, He rarely sees the necessity of letting us know in advance where that path may lead us — this is the very foundation of the concept of faith. Like Greta, we may be faced with an unexpected turn of events in our life that throws us into a panic. I recently had just such a situation when we learned that my husband's chronic (and incurable) illness had reached its final stages. At the time I am writing this, all treatment possibilities have been exhausted and we are moving toward home hospice care and the inevitable end of his life and our life together. By the time you read this I cannot predict what will have transpired but as Oprah would say, here is what I know for sure: God has blessed us with a marriage and a partner-ship and an incredible romance that has lasted for over forty years and the memories of that love story — our story — will comfort me for all the days of my life.

Please contact me via my website (www
.booksbyanna.com) or write to me at P.O.
Box 161, Thiensville, WI 53092. Blessings
and all best wishes to you and yours!!

Anna Schmidt

QUESTIONS FOR DISCUSSION

1. Greta had basically grown up without a mother — her mother having died when she was only three. How has that affected the woman she's turned out to be?

2. In what ways is Lydia a stabilizing influence on Greta and at what cost to her own happiness?

3. What are the differences between Luke and Josef in how they value Greta?

4. What do you think would have happened if Lydia had agreed to allow Luke to court her and they had ended up together?

5. What was the real reason that Luke left Canada?

6. His "sin" was not that he had caused or contributed emotionally to the death of

the woman there. What was the charge brought against him by the father of the woman?

7. How important do you think it was for the congregation to forgive Luke and welcome him back into the fold? Or should the Celery Fields congregation have honored the Ontario congregation's demand that he make things right there before he could be accepted into any other Amish community? Give your reasons for your choice.

8. Given their whirlwind romance and Luke's past and the fact that Josef will continue to be their neighbor in the small community, what are Luke and Greta's chances for a long and happy marriage?

9. What part did faith play in the decisions made and the actions taken by: Greta, Luke, Lydia, Josef?

10. This story is set in the Great Depression of the 1930s — in what ways do you see similarities between those hard times and the hard times Americans have been through most recently?

11. Name three places in this story where God's plan was questioned by one or more characters and three where His plan was followed.

12. In the final book of the AMISH BRIDES OF CELERY FIELDS series, Lydia will indeed find true love. If *you* were writing her story, what would it be?

ABOUT THE AUTHOR

Anna Schmidt is an award-winning author of more than twenty-five works of historical and contemporary fiction. She is a two-time finalist for a coveted RITA® Award from Romance Writers of America, as well as a four-time finalist for an *RT Book Reviews* Reviewer's Choice Award. Her most recent *RT Book Reviews* Reviewer's Choice nomination was for her 2008 Love Inspired Historical novel, *Seaside Cinderella,* which is the first of a series of four historical novels set on the romantic island of Nantucket. Critics have called Anna "a natural writer, spinning tales reminiscent of old favorites like *Miracle on 34th Street.*" Her characters have been called "realistic" and "endearing" and one reviewer raved, "I love Anna Schmidt's style of writing!"